The Black Dwarf

Walter Scott

CONTENTS.

THE BLACK DWARF by Sir Walter Scott, Bart.

I. TALES OF MY LANDLORD

COLLECTED AND REPORTED BY JEDEDIAH CLEISHBOTHAM, SCHOOLMASTER AND PARISH-CLERK OF GANDERCLEUGH.

INTRODUCTION.

As I may, without vanity, presume that the name and official description prefixed to this Proem will secure it, from the sedate and reflecting part of mankind, to whom only I would be understood to address myself, such attention as is due to the sedulous instructor of youth, and the careful performer of my Sabbath duties, I will forbear to hold up a candle to the daylight, or to point out to the judicious those recommendations of my labours which they must necessarily anticipate from the perusal of the title-page. Nevertheless, I am not unaware, that, as Envy always dogs Merit at the heels, there may be those who will whisper, that albeit my learning and good principles cannot (lauded be the heavens) be denied by any one, yet that my situation at Gandercleugh hath been more favourable to my acquisitions in learning than to the enlargement of my views of the ways and works of the present generation. To the which objection, if, peradventure, any such shall be started, my answer shall be threefold:

First, Gandercleugh is, as it were, the central part--the navel (SI FAS SIT DICERE) of this our native realm of Scotland; so that men, from every corner thereof, when travelling on their concernments of business, either towards our metropolis of law, by which I mean Edinburgh, or towards our metropolis and mart of gain, whereby I insinuate Glasgow, are frequently led to make Gandercleugh their abiding stage and place of rest for the night. And it must be acknowledged by the most sceptical, that I, who have sat in the leathern armchair, on the left-hand side of the fire, in the common room of the Wallace Inn, winter and summer, for every evening in my life, during forty years bypast (the Christian Sabbaths only excepted), must have seen more of the manners and customs of various tribes and people, than if I had sought them out by my own painful travel and bodily labour. Even so doth the tollman at the well-frequented turn-pike on the Wellbraehead, sitting at his ease in his own dwelling, gather more receipt of custom, than if, moving forth upon the road, he were to require a contribution from each person whom he chanced to meet in his journey, when, according to the vulgar adage, he might possibly be greeted with more kicks than halfpence.

But, secondly, supposing it again urged, that Ithacus, the most wise of the Greeks, acquired his renown, as the Roman poet hath assured us, by visiting states and men, I reply to the Zoilus who shall adhere to this objection, that, DE FACTO, I have seen states and men also; for I have visited the famous cities of Edinburgh and Glasgow, the former twice, and the latter three times, in the course of my earthly pilgrimage. And, moreover, I had the honour to sit in the General Assembly (meaning, as an auditor, in the galleries thereof), and have heard as much goodly speaking on the law of patronage, as, with the fructification thereof in mine own understanding, hath made me be considered as an oracle upon that doctrine ever since my safe and happy return to Gandercleugh.

Again--and thirdly, If it be nevertheless pretended that my information and knowledge of mankind, however extensive, and however painfully acquired, by constant domestic enquiry, and by foreign travel, is, natheless, incompetent to the task of recording the pleasant narratives of my Landlord, I will let these critics know, to their own eternal shame and confusion as well as to the abashment and discomfiture of all who shall rashly take up a song against me, that I am NOT the writer, redacter, or compiler, of the Tales of my Landlord; nor am I, in one single iota, answerable for their contents, more or less. And now, ye generation of critics, who raise yourselves up as if it were brazen serpents, to hiss with your tongues, and to smite with your stings, bow yourselves down to your native dust, and acknowledge that yours have been the thoughts of ignorance, and the words of vain foolishness. Lo! ye are caught in your own snare, and your own pit hath yawned for you. Turn, then, aside from the task that is too heavy for you; destroy not your teeth by gnawing a file; waste not your strength by spurning against a castle wall; nor spend your breath in contending in swiftness with a fleet steed; and let those weigh the Tales of my Landlord, who shall bring with them the scales of candour cleansed from the rust of prejudice by the hands of intelligent modesty. For these alone they were compiled, as will appear from a brief narrative which my zeal for truth compelled me to make supplementary to the present Proem.

It is well known that my Landlord was a pleasing and a facetious man, acceptable unto all the parish of Gandercleugh, excepting only the Laird, the Exciseman, and those for whom he refused to draw liquor upon trust. Their causes of dislike I will touch separately, adding my own refutation thereof.

His honour, the Laird, accused our Landlord, deceased, of having encouraged, in various times and places, the destruction of hares, rabbits, fowls black and grey, partridges, moor-pouts, roe-deer, and other birds and quadrupeds, at unlawful seasons, and contrary to the laws of this realm, which have secured, in their wisdom, the slaughter of such animals for the great of the earth, whom I have remarked to take an uncommon (though to me, an unintelligible) pleasure therein. Now, in humble deference to his honour, and in justifiable defence of my friend deceased, I reply to this charge, that howsoever the form of such animals might appear to be similar to those so protected by the law, yet it was a mere DECEPTIO VISUS; for what resembled hares were, in fact, HILL-KIDS, and those partaking of the appearance of moor- fowl, were truly WOOD PIGEONS and consumed and eaten EO NOMINE, and not otherwise.

Again, the Exciseman pretended, that my deceased Landlord did encourage that species of manufacture called distillation, without having an especial permission from the Great, technically called a license, for doing so. Now, I stand up to confront this falsehood; and in defiance of him, his gauging-stick, and pen and inkhorn, I tell him, that I never saw, or tasted, a glass of unlawful aqua vitae in the house of my Landlord; nay, that, on the contrary, we needed not such devices, in respect of a pleasing and somewhat seductive liquor, which was vended and consumed at the Wallace Inn, under the name of MOUNTAIN DEW. If there is a penalty against manufacturing such a liquor, let him show me the statute; and when he does, I'll tell him if I will obey it or no.

Concerning those who came to my Landlord for liquor, and went thirsty away, for lack of present coin, or future credit, I cannot but say it has grieved my bowels as if the case had been mine own. Nevertheless, my Landlord considered the necessities of a thirsty soul, and would permit them, in extreme need, and when their soul was impoverished for lack of moisture, to drink to the full value of their watches and wearing apparel, exclusively of their inferior habiliments, which he was uniformly inexorable in obliging them to retain, for the credit of the house. As to mine own part, I may well say, that he never refused me that modicum of refreshment with which I am wont to recruit nature after the fatigues of my school. It is true, I taught his five sons English and Latin, writing, book-keeping, with a tincture of mathematics, and that I instructed his daughter in psalmody. Nor do I remember me of any fee or HONORARIUM received from him on account of these my labours, except the compotations aforesaid. Nevertheless this compensation suited my humour well, since it is a hard sentence to bid a dry throat wait till quarter-day.

But, truly, were I to speak my simple conceit and belief, I think my Landlord was chiefly moved to waive in my behalf the usual requisition of a symbol, or reckoning, from the pleasure he was wont to take in my conversation, which, though solid and edifying in the main, was, like a well-built palace, decorated with facetious narratives and devices, tending much to the enhancement and ornament thereof. And so pleased was my Landlord of the Wallace in his replies during such colloquies, that there was no district in Scotland, yea, and no peculiar, and, as it were, distinctive custom therein practised, but was discussed betwixt us; insomuch, that those who stood by were wont to say, it was worth a bottle of ale to hear us communicate with each other. And not a few travellers, from distant parts, as well as from the remote districts of our kingdom, were wont to mingle in the conversation, and to tell news that had been gathered in foreign lands, or preserved from oblivion in this our own.

Now I chanced to have contracted for teaching the lower classes with a young person called Peter, or Patrick, Pattieson, who had been educated for our Holy Kirk, yea, had, by the license of presbytery, his voice opened therein as a preacher, who delighted in the collection of olden tales and legends, and in garnishing them with the flowers of poesy, whereof he was a vain and frivolous professor. For he followed not the example of those strong poets whom I preposed to him as a pattern, but formed versification of a flimsy and modern texture, to the compounding whereof was necessary small pains and less thought. And hence I have chid him as being one of those who bring forward the fatal revolution prophesied by Mr. Robert Carey, in his Vaticination on the Death of the celebrated Dr. John Donne:

Now thou art gone, and thy strict laws will be Too hard for libertines in poetry; Till verse (by thee refined) in this last age Turn ballad rhyme.

I had also disputations with him touching his indulging rather a flowing and redundant than a concise and stately diction in his prose exercitations. But notwithstanding these symptoms of inferior taste, and a humour of contradicting his betters upon passages of dubious construction in Latin authors, I did grievously lament when Peter Pattieson was removed from me by death, even as if he had been the offspring of my own loins. And in respect his papers had been left in my care (to answer funeral and death-bed expenses), I conceived myself entitled to dispose of one parcel thereof, entitled, "Tales of my Landlord," to one cunning in the trade (as it is called) of bookselling. He was a mirthful man, of small stature, cunning in counterfeiting of voices, and in making facetious tales and responses, and whom I have to laud for the truth of his dealings towards me.

Now, therefore, the world may see the injustice that charges me with incapacity to write these narratives, seeing, that though I have proved that I could have written them if I would, yet, not having done so, the censure will deservedly fall, if at all due, upon the memory of Mr. Peter Pattieson; whereas I must be justly entitled to the praise, when any is due, seeing that, as the Dean of St. Patrick's wittily and logically expresseth it,

That without which a thing is not, Is CAUSA SINE QUA NON.

The work, therefore, is unto me as a child is to a parent; in the which child, if it proveth worthy, the parent hath honour and praise; but, if otherwise, the disgrace will deservedly attach to itself alone.

I have only further to intimate, that Mr. Peter Pattieson, in arranging these Tales for the press, hath more consulted his own fancy than the accuracy of the narrative; nay, that he hath sometimes blended two or three stories together for the mere grace of his plots. Of which infidelity, although I disapprove and enter my testimony against it, yet I have not taken upon me to correct the same, in respect it was the will of the deceased, that his manuscript should be submitted to the press without diminution or alteration. A fanciful nicety it was on the part of my deceased friend, who, if thinking wisely, ought rather to have conjured me, by all the tender ties of our friendship and common pursuits, to have carefully revised, altered, and augmented, at my judgment and discretion. But the will of the dead must be scrupulously obeyed, even when we weep over their pertinacity and self-delusion. So, gentle reader, I bid you farewell, recommending you to such fare as the mountains of your own country produce; and I will only farther premise, that each Tale is preceded by a short introduction, mentioning the persons by whom, and the circumstances under which, the materials thereof were collected.

JEDEDIAH CLEISHBOTHAM.

II. INTRODUCTION to THE BLACK DWARF.

The ideal being who is here presented as residing in solitude, and haunted by a consciousness of his own deformity, and a suspicion of his being generally subjected to the scorn of his fellow-men, is not altogether imaginary. An individual existed many years since, under the author's observation, which suggested such a character. This poor unfortunate man's name was David Ritchie, a native of Tweeddale. He was the son of a labourer in the slate-quarries of Stobo, and must have been born in the misshapen form which he exhibited, though he sometimes imputed it to ill-usage when in infancy. He was bred a brush-maker at Edinburgh, and had wandered to several places, working at his trade, from all which he was chased by the disagreeable attention which his hideous singularity of form and face attracted wherever he came. The author understood him to say he had even been in Dublin.

Tired at length of being the object of shouts, laughter, and derision, David Ritchie resolved, like a deer hunted from the herd, to retreat to some wilderness, where he might have the least possible communication with the world which scoffed at him. He settled himself, with this view, upon a patch of wild moorland at the bottom of a bank on the farm of Woodhouse, in the sequestered vale of the small river Manor, in Peeblesshire. The few people who had occasion to pass that way were much surprised, and some superstitious persons a little alarmed, to see so strange a figure as Bow'd Davie (i.e. Crooked David) employed in a task, for which he seemed so totally unfit, as that of erecting a house. The cottage which he built was extremely small, but the walls, as well as those of a little garden that surrounded it, were constructed with an ambitious degree of solidity, being composed of layers of large stones and turf; and some of the corner stones were so weighty, as to puzzle the spectators how such a person as the architect could possibly have raised them. In fact, David received from passengers, or those who came attracted by curiosity, a good deal of assistance; and as no one knew how much aid had been given by others, the wonder of each individual remained undiminished.

The proprietor of the ground, the late Sir James Naesmith, baronet, chanced to pass this singular dwelling, which, having been placed there without right or leave asked or given, formed an exact parallel with Falstaff's simile of a "fair house built on another's ground;" so that poor David might have lost his edifice by mistaking the property where he had erected it. Of course, the proprietor entertained no idea of exacting such a forfeiture, but readily sanctioned the harmless encroachment.

The personal description of Elshender of Mucklestane-Moor has been generally allowed to be a tolerably exact and unexaggerated portrait of David of Manor Water. He was not quite three feet and a half high, since he could stand upright in the door of his mansion, which was just that height. The following particulars concerning his figure and temper occur in the SCOTS MAGAZINE for 1817, and are now understood to have been communicated by the ingenious Mr. Robert Chambers of Edinburgh, who has recorded with much spirit the traditions of the Good Town, and, in other publications, largely and agreeably added to the stock of our popular antiquities. He is the countryman of David Ritchie, and had the best access to collect anecdotes of him.

"His skull," says this authority, "which was of an oblong and rather unusual shape, was said to be of such strength, that he could strike it with ease through the panel of a door, or the end of a barrel. His laugh is said to have been quite horrible; and his screech-owl voice, shrill, uncouth, and dissonant, corresponded well with his other peculiarities.

"There was nothing very uncommon about his dress. He usually wore an old slouched hat when he went abroad; and when at home, a sort of cowl or night-cap. He never wore shoes, being unable to adapt them to his mis-shapen finlike feet, but always had both feet and legs quite concealed, and wrapt up with pieces of cloth. He always walked with a sort of pole or pike-staff, considerably taller than himself. His habits were, in many respects, singular, and indicated a mind congenial to its uncouth tabernacle. A jealous, misanthropical, and irritable temper, was his prominent characteristic. The sense of his deformity haunted him like a phantom. And the insults and scorn to which this exposed him, had poisoned his heart with fierce and bitter feelings, which, from other points in his character, do not appear to have been more largely infused into his original temperament than that of his fellow-men.

"He detested children, on account of their propensity to insult and persecute him. To strangers he was generally reserved, crabbed, and surly; and though he by no means refused assistance or charity, he seldom either expressed or exhibited much gratitude. Even towards persons who had been his greatest benefactors, and who possessed the greatest share of his good- will, he frequently displayed much caprice and jealousy. A lady who had known him from his infancy, and who has furnished us in the most obliging manner with some particulars respecting him, says, that although Davie showed as much respect and attachment to her father's family, as it was in his nature to show to any, yet they were always obliged to be very cautious in their deportment towards him. One day, having gone to visit him with another lady, he took them through his garden, and was showing them, with much pride and good-humour, all his rich and tastefully assorted borders, when they happened to stop near a plot of cabbages which had been somewhat injured by the caterpillars. Davie, observing one of the ladies smile, instantly assumed his savage, scowling aspect, rushed among the cabbages, and dashed them to pieces with his KENT, exclaiming, 'I hate the worms, for they mock me!'

"Another lady, likewise a friend and old acquaintance of his, very unintentionally gave David mortal offence on a similar occasion. Throwing back his jealous glance as he was ushering her into his garden, he fancied he observed her spit, and exclaimed, with great ferocity, 'Am I a toad, woman! that ye spit at me--that ye spit at me?' and without listening to any answer or excuse, drove her out of his garden with imprecations and insult. When irritated by persons for whom he entertained little respect, his misanthropy displayed itself in words, and sometimes in actions, of still greater rudeness; and he used on such occasions the most unusual and singularly savage imprecations and threats." [SCOTS MAGAZINE, vol. lxxx. p.207.]

Nature maintains a certain balance of good and evil in all her works; and there is no state perhaps so utterly desolate, which does not possess some source of gratification peculiar to itself, This poor man, whose misanthropy was founded in a sense on his own preternatural deformity, had yet his own particular enjoyments. Driven into solitude, he became an admirer of the beauties of nature. His garden, which he sedulously cultivated, and from a piece of wild moorland made a very productive spot, was his pride and his delight; but he was also an admirer of more natural beauty: the soft sweep of the green hill, the bubbling of a clear fountain, or the complexities of a wild thicket, were scenes on which he often gazed for hours, and, as he said, with inexpressible delight. It was perhaps for this reason that he was fond of Shenstone's pastorals, and some parts of PARADISE LOST. The author has heard his most unmusical voice repeat the celebrated description of Paradise, which he seemed fully to appreciate. His other studies were of a different cast, chiefly polemical. He never went to the parish church, and was therefore suspected of entertaining heterodox opinions, though his objection was probably to the concourse of spectators, to whom he must have exposed his unseemly deformity. He spoke of a future state with intense feeling, and even with tears. He expressed disgust at the idea, of his remains being mixed with the common rubbish, as he called it, of the churchyard, and selected with his usual taste a beautiful and wild spot in the glen where he had his hermitage, in which to take his last repose. He changed his mind, however, and was finally interred in the common burial- ground of Manor parish.

The author has invested Wise Elshie with some qualities which made him appear, in the eyes of the vulgar, a man possessed of supernatural power. Common fame paid David Ritchie a similar compliment, for some of the poor and ignorant, as well as all the children, in the neighbourhood, held him to be what is called uncanny. He himself did not altogether discourage the idea; it enlarged his very limited circle of power, and in so far gratified his conceit; and it soothed his misanthropy, by increasing his means of giving terror or pain. But even in a rude Scottish glen thirty years back, the fear of sorcery was very much out of date.

David Ritchie affected to frequent solitary scenes, especially such as were supposed to be haunted, and valued himself upon his courage in doing so. To be sure he had little chance of meeting anything more ugly than himself. At heart, he was superstitious, and planted many rowans (mountain ashes) around his hut, as a certain defence against necromancy. For the same reason, doubtless, he desired to have rowan-trees set above his grave.

We have stated that David Ritchie loved objects of natural beauty. His only living favourites were a dog and a cat, to which he was particularly attached, and his bees, which he treated with great care. He took a sister, latterly, to live in a hut adjacent to his own, but he did not permit her to enter it. She was weak in intellect, but not deformed in person; simple, or rather silly, but not, like her brother, sullen or bizarre. David was never affectionate to her; it was not in his nature; but he endured her. He maintained himself and her by the sale of the product of their garden and bee-hives; and, latterly, they had a small allowance from the parish. Indeed, in the simple and patriarchal state in which the country then was, persons in the situation of David and his sister were sure to be supported. They had only to apply to the next gentleman or respectable farmer, and were sure to find them equally ready and willing to supply their very moderate wants. David often received gratuities from strangers, which he never asked, never refused, and never seemed to consider as an obligation. He had a right, indeed, to regard himself as one of Nature's paupers, to whom she gave a title to be maintained by his kind, even by that deformity which closed against him all ordinary ways of supporting himself by his own labour. Besides, a bag was suspended in the mill for David Ritchie's benefit; and those who were carrying home a melder of meal, seldom failed to add a GOWPEN [Handful] to the alms-bag of the deformed cripple. In short, David had no occasion for money, save to purchase snuff, his only luxury, in which he indulged himself liberally. When he died, in the beginning of the present century, he was found to have hoarded about twenty pounds, a habit very consistent with his disposition; for wealth is power, and power was what David Ritchie desired to possess, as a compensation for his exclusion from human society.

His sister survived till the publication of the tale to which this brief notice forms the introduction; and the author is sorry to learn that a sort of "local sympathy," and the curiosity then expressed concerning the Author of WAVERLEY and the subjects of his Novels, exposed the poor woman to enquiries which gave her pain. When pressed about her brother's peculiarities, she asked, in her turn, why they would not permit the dead to rest? To others, who pressed for some account of her parents, she answered in the same tone of feeling.

The author saw this poor, and, it may be said, unhappy man, in autumn 1797 being then, as he has the happiness still to remain, connected by ties of intimate friendship with the family of the venerable Dr. Adam Fergusson, the philosopher and historian, who then resided at the mansion-house of Halyards, in the vale of Manor, about a mile from Ritchie's hermitage, the author was upon a visit at Halyards, which lasted for several days, and was made acquainted with this singular anchorite, whom Dr. Fergusson considered as an extraordinary character, and whom he assisted in various ways, particularly by the occasional loan of books. Though the taste of the philosopher and the poor peasant did not, it may be supposed, always correspond, [I remember David was particularly anxious to see a book, which he called, I think, LETTERS TO ELECT LADIES, and which, he said, was the best composition he had ever read; but Dr. Fergusson's library did not supply the volume.] Dr. Fergusson considered him as a man of a powerful capacity and original ideas, but whose mind was thrown off its just bias by a predominant degree of self-love and self- opinion, galled by the sense of ridicule and contempt, and avenging itself upon society, in idea at least, by a gloomy misanthropy.

David Ritchie, besides the utter obscurity of his life while in existence, had been dead for many years, when it occurred to the author that such a character might be made a powerful agent in fictitious narrative. He, accordingly, sketched that of Elshie of the Mucklestane-Moor. The story was intended to be longer, and the catastrophe more artificially brought out; but a friendly critic, to whose opinion I subjected the work in its progress, was of opinion, that the idea of the Solitary was of a kind too revolting, and more likely to disgust than to interest the reader. As I had good right to consider my adviser as an excellent judge of public opinion, I got off my subject by hastening the story to an end, as fast as it was possible; and, by huddling into one volume, a tale which was designed to occupy two, have perhaps produced a narrative as much disproportioned and distorted, as the Black Dwarf who is its subject.

*

III. THE BLACK DWARF.

CHAPTER I.

PRELIMINARY.

Hast any philosophy in thee, Shepherd? AS YOU LIKE IT.

It was a fine April morning (excepting that it had snowed hard the night before, and the ground remained covered with a dazzling mantle of six inches in depth) when two horsemen rode up to the Wallace Inn. The first was a strong, tall, powerful man, in a grey riding-coat, having a hat covered with waxcloth, a huge silver-mounted horsewhip, boots, and dreadnought overalls. He was mounted on a large strong brown mare, rough in coat, but well in condition, with a saddle of the yeomanry cut, and a double- bitted military bridle. The man who accompanied him was apparently his servant; he rode a shaggy little grey pony, had a blue bonnet on his head, and a large check napkin folded about his neck, wore a pair of long blue worsted hose instead of boots, had his gloveless hands much stained with tar, and observed an air of deference and respect towards his companion, but without any of those indications of precedence and punctilio which are preserved between the gentry and their domestics. On the contrary, the two travellers entered the court-yard abreast, and the concluding sentence of the conversation which had been carrying on betwixt them was a joint ejaculation, "Lord guide us, an this weather last, what will come o' the lambs!" The hint was sufficient for my Landlord, who, advancing to take the horse of the principal person, and holding him by the reins as he dismounted, while his ostler rendered the same service to the attendant, welcomed the stranger to Gandercleugh, and, in the same breath, enquired, "What news from the south hielands?"

"News?" said the farmer, "bad eneugh news, I think;--an we can carry through the yowes, it will be a' we can do; we maun e'en leave the lambs to the Black Dwarfs care."

"Ay, ay," subjoined the old shepherd (for such he was), shaking his head, "he'll be unco busy amang the morts this season."

"The Black Dwarf!" said MY LEARNED FRIEND AND PATRON, Mr. Jedediah Cleishbotham, "and what sort of a personage may he be?"

[We have, in this and other instances, printed in italics (CAPITALS in this etext) some few words which the worthy editor, Mr. Jedediah Cleishbotham, seems to have interpolated upon the text of his deceased friend, Mr. Pattieson. We must observe, once for all, that such liberties seem only to have been taken by the learned gentleman where his own character and conduct are concerned; and surely he must be the best judge of the style in which his own character and conduct should be treated of.]

"Hout awa, man," answered the farmer, "ye'll hae heard o' Canny Elshie the Black Dwarf, or I am muckle mistaen--A' the warld tells tales about him, but it's but daft nonsense after a'--I dinna believe a word o't frae beginning to end."

"Your father believed it unco stievely, though," said the old man, to whom the scepticism of his master gave obvious displeasure.

"Ay, very true, Bauldie, but that was in the time o' the blackfaces-- they believed a hantle queer things in thae days, that naebody heeds since the lang sheep cam in."

"The mair's the pity, the mair's the pity," said the old man. "Your father, and sae I have aften tell'd ye, maister, wad hae been sair vexed to hae seen the auld peel-house wa's pu'd down to make park dykes; and the bonny broomy knowe, where he liked sae weel to sit at e'en, wi' his plaid about him, and look at the kye as they cam down the loaning, ill wad he hae liked to hae seen that braw sunny knowe a' riven out wi' the pleugh in the fashion it is at this day."

"Hout, Bauldie," replied the principal, "tak ye that dram the landlord's offering ye, and never fash your head about the changes o' the warld, sae lang as ye're blithe and bien yoursell."

"Wussing your health, sirs," said the shepherd; and having taken off his glass, and observed the whisky was the right thing, he continued, "It's no for the like o' us to be judging, to be sure; but it was a bonny knowe that broomy knowe, and an unco braw shelter for the lambs in a severe morning like this."

"Ay," said his patron, "but ye ken we maun hae turnips for the lang sheep, billie, and muckle hard wark to get them, baith wi' the pleugh and the howe; and that wad sort ill wi' sitting on the broomy knowe, and cracking about Black Dwarfs, and siccan clavers, as was the gate lang syne, when the short sheep were in the fashion."

"Aweel, aweel, maister," said the attendant, "short sheep had short rents, I'm thinking."

Here my WORTHY AND LEARNED patron again interposed, and observed, "that he could never perceive any material difference, in point of longitude, between one sheep and another."

This occasioned a loud hoarse laugh on the part of the farmer, and an astonished stare on the part of the shepherd.

"It's the woo', man,--it's the woo', and no the beasts themsells, that makes them be ca'd lang or short. I believe if ye were to measure their backs, the short sheep wad be rather the langer- bodied o' the twa; but it's the woo' that pays the rent in thae days, and it had muckle need."

"Odd, Bauldie says very true,--short sheep did make short rents-- my father paid for our steading just threescore punds, and it stands me in three hundred, plack and bawbee.--And that's very true--I hae nae time to be standing here clavering--Landlord, get us our breakfast, and see an' get the yauds fed--I am for doun to Christy Wilson's, to see if him and me can gree about the luckpenny I am to gie him for his year-aulds. We had drank sax mutchkins to the making the bargain at St. Boswell's fair, and some gate we canna gree upon the particulars preeesely, for as muckle time as we took about it--I doubt we draw to a plea--But hear ye, neighbour," addressing my WORTHY AND LEARNED patron, "if ye want to hear onything about lang or short sheep, I will be back here to my kail against ane o'clock; or, if ye want ony auld-warld stories about the Black Dwarf, and sic-like, if ye'll ware a half mutchkin upon Bauldie there, he'll crack t'ye like a pen-gun. And I'se gie ye a mutchkin mysell, man, if I can settle weel wi' Christy Wilson."

The farmer returned at the hour appointed, and with him came Christy Wilson, their difference having been fortunately settled without an appeal to the gentlemen of the long robe. My LEARNED AND WORTHY patron failed not to attend, both on account of the refreshment promised to the mind and to the body, ALTHOUGH HE IS KNOWN TO PARTAKE OF THE LATTER IN A VERY MODERATE DEGREE; and the party, with which my Landlord was associated, continued to sit late in the evening, seasoning their liquor with many choice tales and songs. The last incident which I recollect, was my LEARNED AND WORTHY patron falling from his chair, just as he concluded a long lecture upon temperance, by reciting, from the "Gentle Shepherd," a couplet, which he RIGHT HAPPILY transferred from the vice of avarice to that of ebriety:

He that has just eneugh may soundly sleep, The owercome only fashes folk to keep.

In the course of the evening the Black Dwarf had not been forgotten, and the old shepherd, Bauldie, told so many stories of him, that they excited a good deal of interest. It also appeared, though not till the third punch-bowl was emptied, that much of the farmer's scepticism on the subject was affected, as evincing a liberality of thinking, and a freedom from ancient prejudices, becoming a man who paid three hundred pounds a-year of rent, while, in fact, he had a lurking belief in the traditions of his forefathers. After my usual manner, I made farther enquiries of other persons connected with the wild and pastoral district in which the scene of the following narrative is placed, and I was fortunate enough to recover many links of the story, not generally known, and which account, at least in some degree, for the circumstances of exaggerated marvel with which superstition has attired it in the more vulgar traditions.

[The Black Dwarf, now almost forgotten, was once held a formidable personage by the dalesmen of the Border, where he got the blame of whatever mischief befell the sheep or cattle. "He was," says Dr. Leyden, who makes considerable use of him in the ballad called the Cowt of Keeldar, "a fairy of the most malignant order--the genuine Northern Duergar." The best and most authentic account of this dangerous and mysterious being occurs in a tale communicated to the author by that eminent antiquary, Richard Surtees, Esq. of Mainsforth, author of the HISTORY OF THE BISHOPRIC OF DURHAM.

According to this well-attested legend, two young Northumbrians were out on a shooting party, and had plunged deep among the mountainous moorlands which border on Cumberland. They stopped for refreshment in a little secluded dell by the side of a rivulet. There, after they had partaken of such food as they brought with them, one of the party fell asleep; the other, unwilling to disturb his friend's repose, stole silently out of the dell with the purpose of looking around him, when he was astonished to find himself close to a being who seemed not to belong to this world, as he was the most hideous dwarf that the sun had ever shone on. His head was of full human size, forming a frightful contrast with his height, which was considerably under four feet. It was thatched with no other covering than long matted red hair, like that of the felt of a badger in consistence, and in colour a reddish brown, like the hue of the heather-blossom. His limbs seemed of great strength; nor was he otherwise deformed than from their undue proportion in thickness to his diminutive height. The terrified sportsman stood gazing on this horrible apparition, until, with an angry countenance, the being demanded by what right he intruded himself on those hills, and destroyed their harmless inhabitants. The perplexed stranger endeavoured to propitiate the incensed dwarf, by offering to surrender his game, as he would to an earthly Lord of the Manor. The proposal only redoubled the offence already taken by the dwarf, who alleged that he was the lord of those mountains, and the protector of the wild creatures who found a retreat in their solitary recesses; and that all spoils derived from their death, or misery, were abhorrent to him. The hunter humbled himself before the angry goblin, and by protestations of his ignorance, and of his resolution to abstain from such intrusion in future, at last succeeded in pacifying him. The gnome now became more communicative, and spoke of himself as belonging to a species of beings something between the angelic race and humanity. He added, moreover, which could hardly have been anticipated, that he had hopes of sharing in the redemption of the race of Adam. He pressed the sportsman to visit his dwelling, which he said was hard by, and plighted his faith for his safe return. But at this moment, the shout of the sportsman's companion was heard calling for his friend, and the dwarf, as if unwilling that more than one person should be cognisant of his presence, disappeared as the young man emerged from the dell to join his comrade.

It was the universal opinion of those most experienced in such matters, that if the shooter had accompanied the spirit, he would, notwithstanding the dwarf's fair pretences, have been either torn to pieces, or immured for years in the recesses of some fairy hill.

Such is the last and most authentic account of the apparition of the Black Dwarf.]

CHAPTER II.

Will none but Hearne the Hunter serve your turn? MERRY WIVES OF WINDSOR.

In one of the most remote districts of the south of Scotland, where an ideal line, drawn along the tops of lofty and bleak mountains, separates that land from her sister kingdom, a young man, called Halbert, or Hobbie Elliot, a substantial farmer, who boasted his descent from old Martin Elliot of the Preakin-tower, noted in Border story and song, was on his return from deer- stalking. The deer, once so numerous among these solitary wastes, were now reduced to a very few herds, which, sheltering themselves in the most remote and inaccessible recesses, rendered the task of pursuing them equally toilsome and precarious. There were, however, found many youth of the country ardently attached to this sport, with all its dangers and fatigues. The sword had been sheathed upon the Borders for more than a hundred years, by the peaceful union of the crowns in the reign of James the First of Great Britain. Still the country retained traces of what it had been in former days; the inhabitants, their more peaceful avocations having been repeatedly interrupted by the civil wars of the preceding century, were scarce yet broken in to the habits of regular industry, sheep-farming had not been introduced upon any considerable scale, and the feeding of black cattle was the chief purpose to which the hills and valleys were applied. Near to the farmer's house, the tenant usually contrived to raise such a crop of oats or barley, as afforded meal for his family; and the whole of this slovenly and imperfect mode of cultivation left much time upon his own hands, and those of his domestics. This was usually employed by the young men in hunting and fishing; and the spirit of adventure, which formerly led to raids and forays in the same districts, was still to be discovered in the eagerness with which they pursued those rural sports.

The more high-spirited among the youth were, about the time that our narrative begins, expecting, rather with hope than apprehension, an opportunity of emulating their fathers in their military achievements, the recital of which formed the chief part of their amusement within doors. The passing of the Scottish act of security had given the alarm of England, as it seemed to point at a separation of the two British kingdoms, after the decease of Queen Anne, the reigning sovereign. Godolphin, then at the head of the English administration, foresaw that there was no other mode of avoiding the probable extremity of a civil war, but by carrying through an incorporating union. How that treaty was managed, and how little it seemed for some time to promise the beneficial results which have since taken place to such extent, may be learned from the history of the period. It is enough for our purpose to say, that all Scotland was indignant at the terms on which their legislature had surrendered their national independence. The general resentment led to the strangest leagues and to the wildest plans. The Cameronians were about to take arms for the restoration of the house of Stewart, whom they regarded, with justice, as their oppressors; and the intrigues of the period presented the strange picture of papists, prelatists, and presbyterians, caballing among themselves against the English government, out of a common feeling that their country had been treated with injustice. The fermentation was universal; and, as the population of Scotland had been generally trained to arms, under the act of security, they were not indifferently prepared for war, and waited but the declaration of some of the nobility to break out into open hostility. It was at this period of public confusion that our story opens.

The cleugh, or wild ravine, into which Hobbie Elliot had followed the game, was already far behind him, and he was considerably advanced on his return homeward, when the night began to close upon him. This would have been a circumstance of great indifference to the experienced sportsman, who could have walked blindfold over every inch of his native heaths, had it not happened near a spot, which, according to the traditions of the country, was in extremely bad fame, as haunted by supernatural appearances. To tales of this kind Hobbie had, from his childhood, lent an attentive ear; and as no part of the country afforded such a variety of legends, so no man was more deeply read in their fearful lore than Hobbie of the Heugh-foot; for so our gallant was called, to distinguish him from a round dozen of Elliots who bore the same Christian name. It cost him no efforts, therefore, to call to memory the terrific incidents connected with the extensive waste upon which he was now entering. In fact, they presented themselves with a readiness which he felt to be somewhat dismaying.

This dreary common was called Mucklestane-Moor, from a huge column of unhewn granite, which raised its massy head on a knell near the centre of the heath, perhaps to tell of the mighty dead who slept beneath, or to preserve the memory of some bloody skirmish. The real cause of its existence had, however, passed away; and tradition, which is as frequently an inventor of fiction as a preserver of truth, had supplied its place with a supplementary legend of her own, which now came full upon Hobbie's memory. The ground about the pillar was strewed, or rather encumbered, with many large fragments of stone of the same consistence with the column, which, from their appearance as they lay scattered on the waste, were popularly called the Grey Geese of Mucklestane-Moor. The legend accounted for this name and appearance by the catastrophe of a noted and most formidable witch who frequented these hills in former days, causing the ewes to KEB, and the kine to cast their calves, and performing all the feats of mischief ascribed to these evil beings. On this moor she used to hold her revels with her sister hags; and rings were still pointed out on which no grass nor heath ever grew, the turf being, as it were, calcined by the scorching hoofs of their diabolical partners.

Once upon a time this old hag is said to have crossed the moor, driving before her a flock of geese, which she proposed to sell to advantage at a neighbouring fair;--for it is well known that the fiend, however liberal in imparting his powers of doing mischief, ungenerously leaves his allies under the necessity of performing the meanest rustic labours for subsistence. The day was far advanced, and her chance of obtaining a good price depended on her being first at the market. But the geese, which had hitherto preceded her in a pretty orderly manner, when they came to this wide common, interspersed with marshes and pools of water, scattered in every direction, to plunge into the element in which they delighted. Incensed at the obstinacy with which they defied all her efforts to collect them, and not remembering the precise terms of the contract by which the fiend was bound to obey her commands for a certain space, the sorceress exclaimed, "Deevil, that neither I nor they ever stir from this spot more!" The words were hardly uttered, when, by a metamorphosis as sudden as any in Ovid, the hag and her refractory flock were converted into stone, the angel whom she served, being a strict formalist, grasping eagerly at an opportunity of completing the ruin of her body and soul by a literal obedience to her orders. It is said, that when she perceived and felt the transformation which was about to take place, she exclaimed to the treacherous fiend, "Ah, thou false thief! lang hast thou promised me a grey gown, and now I am getting ane that will last for ever." The dimensions of the pillar, and of the stones, were often appealed to, as a proof of the superior stature and size of old women and geese in the days of other years, by those praisers of the past who held the comfortable opinion of the gradual degeneracy of mankind.

All particulars of this legend Hobbie called to mind as he passed along the moor. He also remembered, that, since the catastrophe had taken place, the scene of it had been avoided, at least after night-fall, by all human beings, as being the ordinary resort of kelpies, spunkies, and other demons, once the companions of the witch's diabolical revels, and now continuing to rendezvous upon the same spot, as if still in attendance on their transformed mistress. Hobbie's natural hardihood, however, manfully combated with these intrusive sensations of awe. He summoned to his side the brace of large greyhounds, who were the companions of his sports, and who were wont, in his own phrase, to fear neither dog nor devil; he looked at the priming of his piece, and, like the clown in Hallowe'en, whistled up the warlike ditty of Jock of the Side, as a general causes his drums be beat to inspirit the doubtful courage of his soldiers.

In this state of mind, he was very glad to hear a friendly voice shout in his rear, and propose to him a partner on the road. He slackened his pace, and was quickly joined by a youth well known to him, a gentleman of some fortune in that remote country, and who had been abroad on the same errand with himself. Young Earnscliff, "of that ilk," had lately come of age, and succeeded to a moderate fortune, a good deal dilapidated, from the share his family had taken in the disturbances of the period. They were much and generally respected in the country; a reputation which this young gentleman seemed likely to sustain, as he was well educated, and of excellent dispositions.

"Now, Earnscliff;" exclaimed Hobbie, "I am glad to meet your honour ony gate, and company's blithe on a bare moor like this --it's an unco bogilly bit--Where hae ye been sporting?"

"Up the Carla Cleugh, Hobbie," answered Earnscliff, returning his greeting. "But will our dogs keep the peace, think you?"

"Deil a fear o' mine," said Hobbie, "they hae scarce a leg to stand on.--Odd! the deer's fled the country, I think! I have been as far as Inger-fell-foot, and deil a horn has Hobbie seen, excepting three red-wud raes, that never let me within shot of them, though I gaed a mile round to get up the wind to them, an' a'. Deil o' me wad care muckle, only I wanted some venison to our auld gude-dame. The carline, she sits in the neuk yonder, upbye, and cracks about the grand shooters and hunters lang syne --Odd, I think they hae killed a' the deer in the country, for my part."

"Well, Hobbie, I have shot a fat buck, and sent him to Earnscliff this morning--you shall have half of him for your grandmother."

"Mony thanks to ye, Mr. Patrick, ye're kend to a' the country for a kind heart. It will do the auld wife's heart gude--mair by token, when she kens it comes frae you--and maist of a' gin ye'll come up and take your share, for I reckon ye are lonesome now in the auld tower, and a' your folk at that weary Edinburgh. I wonder what they can find to do amang a wheen ranks o' stane- houses wi' slate on the tap o' them, that might live on their ain bonny green hills."

"My education and my sisters' has kept my mother much in Edinburgh for several years," said Earnscliff; "but I promise you I propose to make up for lost time."

"And ye'll rig out the auld tower a bit," said Hobbie, "and live hearty and neighbour-like wi' the auld family friends, as the Laird o' Earnscliff should? I can tell ye, my mother--my grandmother I mean--but, since we lost our ain mother, we ca' her sometimes the tane, and sometimes the tother--but, ony gate, she conceits hersell no that distant connected wi' you."

"Very true, Hobbie, and I will come to the Heugh-foot to dinner to-morrow with all my heart."

"Weel, that's kindly said! We are auld neighbours, an we were nae kin--and my gude-dame's fain to see you--she clavers about your father that was killed lang syne."

"Hush, hush, Hobbie--not a word about that--it's a story better forgotten."

"I dinna ken--if it had chanced amang our folk, we wad hae keepit it in mind mony a day till we got some mends for't--but ye ken your ain ways best, you lairds--I have heard say that Ellieslaw's friend stickit your sire after the laird himsell had mastered his sword."

"Fie, fie, Hobbie; it was a foolish brawl, occasioned by wine and politics--many swords were drawn--it is impossible to say who struck the blow."

"At ony rate, auld Ellieslaw was aiding and abetting; and I am sure if ye were sae disposed as to take amends on him, naebody could say it was wrang, for your father's blood is beneath his nails--and besides there's naebody else left that was concerned to take amends upon, and he's a prelatist and a jacobite into the bargain--I can tell ye the country folk look for something atween ye."

"O for shame, Hobbie!" replied the young Laird; "you, that profess religion, to stir your friend up to break the law, and take vengeance at his own hand, and in such a bogilly bit too, where we know not what beings may be listening to us!"

"Hush, hush!" said Hobbie, drawing nearer to his companion, "I was nae thinking o' the like o' them--But I can guess a wee bit what keeps your hand up, Mr. Patrick; we a' ken it's no lack o' courage, but the twa grey een of a bonny lass, Miss Isabel Vere, that keeps you sae sober."

"I assure you, Hobbie," said his companion, rather angrily, "I assure you you are mistaken; and it is extremely wrong of you, either to think of, or to utter, such an idea; I have no idea of permitting freedoms to be carried so far as to connect my name with that of any young lady."

"Why, there now--there now!" retorted Elliot; "did I not say it was nae want o' spunk that made ye sae mim?--Weel, weel, I meant nae offence; but there's just ae thing ye may notice frae a friend. The auld Laird of Ellieslaw has the auld riding blood far hetter at his heart than ye hae--troth, he kens naething about thae newfangled notions o' peace and quietness--he's a' for the auld-warld doings o' lifting and laying on, and he has a wheen stout lads at his back too, and keeps them weel up in heart, and as fu' o' mischief as young colts. Where he gets the gear to do't nane can say; he lives high, and far abune his rents here; however, he pays his way--Sae, if there's ony out-break in the country, he's likely to break out wi' the first--and weel does he mind the auld quarrels between ye, I'm surmizing he'll be for a touch at the auld tower at Earnscliff."

"Well, Hobbie," answered the young gentleman, "if he should be so ill advised, I shall try to make the old tower good against him, as it has been made good by my betters against his betters many a day ago."

"Very right--very right--that's speaking like a man now," said the stout yeoman; "and, if sae should be that this be sae, if ye'll just gar your servant jow out the great bell in the tower, there's me, and my twa brothers, and little Davie of the Stenhouse, will be wi' you, wi' a' the power we can make, in the snapping of a flint."

"Many thanks, Hobbie," answered Earnscliff; "but I hope we shall have no war of so unnatural and unchristian a kind in our time."

"Hout, sir, hout," replied Elliot; "it wad be but a wee bit neighbour war, and Heaven and earth would make allowances for it in this uncultivated place--it's just the nature o' the folk and the land--we canna live quiet like Loudon folk--we haena sae muckle to do. It's impossible."

"Well, Hobbie," said the Laird, "for one who believes so deeply as you do in supernatural appearances, I must own you take Heaven in your own hand rather audaciously, considering where we are walking."

"What needs I care for the Mucklestane-Moor ony mair than ye do yoursell, Earnscliff?" said Hobbie, something offended; "to be sure, they do say there's a sort o' worricows and lang-nebbit things about the land, but what need I care for them? I hae a good conscience, and little to answer for, unless it be about a rant amang the lasses, or a splore at a fair, and that's no muckle to speak of. Though I say it mysell, I am as quiet a lad and as peaceable--"

"And Dick Turnbull's head that you broke, and Willie of Winton whom you shot at?" said his travelling companion.

"Hout, Earnscliff, ye keep a record of a' men's misdoings --Dick's head's healed again, and we're to fight out the quarrel at Jeddart, on the Rood-day, so that's like a thing settled in a peaceable way; and then I am friends wi' Willie again, puir child--it was but twa or three hail draps after a'. I wad let onybody do the like o't to me for a pint o' brandy. But Willie's lowland bred, poor fallow, and soon frighted for himsell--And, for the worricows, were we to meet ane on this very bit--"

"As is not unlikely," said young Earnscliff, "for there stands your old witch, Hobbie."

"I say," continued Elliot, as if indignant at this hint--"I say, if the auld carline hersell was to get up out o' the grund just before us here, I would think nae mair--But, gude preserve us, Earnscliff; what can yon, be!"

CHAPTER III.

Brown Dwarf, that o'er the moorland strays, Thy name to Keeldar tell! "The Brown Man of the Moor, that stays Beneath the heather-bell." JOHN LEYDEN

The object which alarmed the young farmer in the middle of his valorous protestations, startled for a moment even his less prejudiced companion. The moon, which had arisen during their conversation, was, in the phrase of that country, wading or struggling with clouds, and shed only a doubtful and occasional light. By one of her beams, which streamed upon the great granite column to which they now approached, they discovered a form, apparently human, but of a size much less than ordinary, which moved slowly among the large grey stones, not like a person intending to journey onward, but with the slow, irregular, flitting movement of a being who hovers around some spot of melancholy recollection, uttering also, from time to time, a sort of indistinct muttering sound. This so much resembled his idea of the motions of an apparition, that Hobbie Elliot, making a dead pause, while his hair erected itself upon his scalp, whispered to his companion, "It's Auld Ailie hersell! Shall I gie her a shot, in the name of God?"

"For Heaven's sake, no," said his companion, holding down the weapon which he was about to raise to the aim--"for Heaven's sake, no; it's some poor distracted creature."

"Ye're distracted yoursell, for thinking of going so near to her," said Elliot, holding his companion in his turn, as he prepared to advance. "We'll aye hae time to pit ower a bit prayer (an I could but mind ane) afore she comes this length --God! she's in nae hurry," continued he, growing bolder from his companion's confidence, and the little notice the apparition seemed to take of them. "She hirples like a hen on a het girdle. I redd ye, Earnscliff" (this he added in a gentle whisper), "let us take a cast about, as if to draw the wind on a buck-- the bog is no abune knee-deep, and better a saft road as bad company." [The Scots use the epithet soft, IN MALAM PARTEM, in two cases, at least. A SOFT road is a road through quagmire and bogs; and SOFT weather signifies that which is very rainy.]

Earnscliff, however, in spite of his companion's resistance and remonstrances, continued to advance on the path they had originally pursued, and soon confronted the object of their investigation.

The height of the figure, which appeared even to decrease as they approached it, seemed to be under four feet, and its form, as far as the imperfect light afforded them the means of discerning, was very nearly as broad as long, or rather of a spherical shape, which could only be occasioned by some strange personal deformity. The young sportsman hailed this extraordinary appearance twice, without receiving any answer, or attending to the pinches by which his companion endeavoured to intimate that their best course was to walk on, without giving farther disturbance to a being of such singular and preternatural exterior. To the third repeated demand of "Who are you? What do you here at this hour of night?"--a voice replied, whose shrill, uncouth, and dissonant tones made Elliot step two paces back, and startled even his companion, "Pass on your way, and ask nought at them that ask nought at you."

"What do you do here so far from shelter? Are you benighted on your journey? Will you follow us home ('God forbid!' ejaculated Hobbie Elliot, involuntarily), and I will give you a lodging?"

"I would sooner lodge by mysell in the deepest of the Tarras- flow," again whispered Hobbie.

"Pass on your way," rejoined the figure, the harsh tones of his voice still more exalted by passion. "I want not your guidance --I want not your lodging--it is five years since my head was under a human roof, and I trust it was for the last time."

"He is mad," said Earnscliff.

"He has a look of auld Humphrey Ettercap, the tinkler, that perished in this very moss about five years syne," answered his superstitious companion; "but Humphrey wasna that awfu' big in the bouk."

"Pass on your way," reiterated the object of their curiosity, "the breath of your human bodies poisons the air around me--the sound of pour human voices goes through my ears like sharp bodkins"

"Lord safe us!" whispered Hobbie, "that the dead should bear sie fearfu' ill-will to the living!--his saul maun be in a puir way, I'm jealous."

"Come, my friend," said Earnscliff, "you seem to suffer under some strong affliction; common humanity will not allow us to leave you here."

"Common humanity!" exclaimed the being, with a scornful laugh that sounded like a shriek, "where got ye that catch-word--that noose for woodcocks--that common disguise for man-traps--that bait which the wretched idiot who swallows, will soon find covers a hook with barbs ten times sharper than those you lay for the animals which you murder for your luxury!"

"I tell you, my friend," again replied Earnscliff, "you are incapable of judging of your own situation--you will perish in this wilderness, and we must, in compassion, force you along with us."

"I'll hae neither hand nor foot in't," said Hobbie; "let the ghaist take his ain way, for God's sake!"

"My blood be on my own head, if I perish here," said the figure; and, observing Earnscliff meditating to lay hold on him, he added, "And your blood be upon yours, if you touch but the skirt of my garments, to infect me with the taint of mortality!"

The moon shone more brightly as he spoke thus, and Earnscliff observed that he held out his right hand armed with some weapon of offence, which glittered in the cold ray like the blade of a long knife, or the barrel of a pistol. It would have been madness to persevere in his attempt upon a being thus armed, and holding such desperate language, especially as it was plain he would have little aid from his companion, who had fairly left him to settle matters with the apparition as he could, and had proceeded a few paces on his way homeward. Earnscliff, however, turned and followed Hobbie, after looking back towards the supposed maniac, who, as if raised to frenzy by the interview, roamed wildly around the great stone, exhausting his voice in shrieks and imprecations, that thrilled wildly along the waste heath.

The two sportsmen moved on some time in silence, until they were out of hearing of these uncouth sounds, which was not ere they had gained a considerable distance from the pillar that gave name to the moor. Each made his private comments on the scene they had witnessed, until Hobbie Elliot suddenly exclaimed, "Weel, I'll uphaud that yon ghaist, if it be a ghaist, has baith done and suffered muckle evil in the flesh, that gars him rampauge in that way after he is dead and gane."

"It seems to me the very madness of misanthropy," said Earnscliff; following his own current of thought.

"And ye didna think it was a spiritual creature, then?" asked Hobbie at his companion.

"Who, I?--No, surely."

"Weel, I am partly of the mind mysell that it may be a live thing--and yet I dinna ken, I wadna wish to see ony thing look liker a bogle."

"At any rate," said Earnscliff, "I will ride over to-morrow and see what has become of the unhappy being."

"In fair daylight?" queried the yeoman; "then, grace o' God, I'se be wi' ye. But here we are nearer to Heugh-foot than to your house by twa mile,--hadna ye better e'en gae hame wi' me, and we'll send the callant on the powny to tell them that you are wi' us, though I believe there's naebody at hame to wait for you but the servants and the cat."

"Have with you then, friend Hobbie," said the young hunter; "and as I would not willingly have either the servants be anxious, or puss forfeit her supper, in my absence, I'll be obliged to you to send the boy as you propose."

"Aweel, that IS kind, I must say. And ye'll gae hame to Heugh- foot? They'll be right blithe to see you, that will they."

This affair settled, they walked briskly on a little farther, when, coming to the ridge of a pretty steep hill, Hobbie Elliot exclaimed, "Now, Earnscliff, I am aye glad when I come to this very bit--Ye see the light below, that's in the ha' window, where grannie, the gash auld carline, is sitting birling at her wheel --and ye see yon other light that's gaun whiddin' back and forrit through amang the windows? that's my cousin, Grace Armstrong, --she's twice as clever about the house as my sisters, and sae they say themsells, for they're good-natured lasses as ever trode on heather; but they confess themsells, and sae does grannie, that she has far maist action, and is the best goer about the toun, now that grannie is off the foot hersell.-

-My brothers, ane o' them's away to wait upon the chamberlain, and ane's at Moss- phadraig, that's our led farm--he can see after the stock just as weel as I can do."

"You are lucky, my good friend, in having so many valuable relations."

"Troth am I--Grace make me thankful, I'se never deny it.--But will ye tell me now, Earnscliff, you that have been at college, and the high-school of Edinburgh, and got a' sort o' lair where it was to be best gotten--will ye tell me--no that it's ony concern of mine in particular,--but I heard the priest of St. John's, and our minister, bargaining about it at the Winter fair, and troth they baith spak very weel--Now, the priest says it's unlawful to marry ane's cousin; but I cannot say I thought he brought out the Gospel authorities half sae weel as our minister- -our minister is thought the best divine and the best preacher atween this and Edinburgh--Dinna ye think he was likely to be right?"

"Certainly marriage, by all protestant Christians, is held to be as free as God made it by the Levitical law; so, Hobbie, there can be no bar, legal or religious, betwixt you and Miss Armstrong."

"Hout awa' wi' your joking, Earnscliff," replied his companion, --" ye are angry aneugh yoursell if ane touches you a bit, man, on the sooth side of the jest--No that I was asking the question about Grace, for ye maun ken she's no my cousin-germain out and out, but the daughter of my uncle;s wife by her first marriage, so she's nae kith nor kin to me--only a connexion like. But now we're at the Sheeling-hill--I'll fire off my gun, to let them ken I'm coming, that's aye my way; and if I hae a deer I gie them twa shots, ane for the deer and ane for mysell."

He fired off his piece accordingly, and the number of lights were seen to traverse the house, and even to gleam before it. Hobbie Elliot pointed out one of these to Earnscliff, which seemed to glide from the house towards some of the outhouses-"That's Grace hersell," said Hobbie. "She'll no meet me at the door, I'se warrant her--but she'll be awa', for a' that, to see if my hounds' supper be ready, poor beasts."

"Love me, love my dog," answered Earnscliff. "Ah, Hobbie, you are a lucky young fellow!"

This observation was uttered with something like a sigh, which apparently did not escape the ear of his companion.

"Hout, other folk may be as lucky as I am--O how I have seen Miss Isabel Vere's head turn after somebody when they passed ane another at the Carlisle races! Wha kens but things may come round in this world?"

Earnscliff muttered something like an answer; but whether in assent of the proposition, or rebuking the application of it, could not easily be discovered; and it seems probable that the speaker himself was willing his meaning should rest in doubt and obscurity. They had now descended the broad loaning, which, winding round the foot of the steep bank, or heugh, brought them in front of the thatched, but comfortable, farm-house, which was the dwelling of Hobbie Elliot and his family.

The doorway was thronged with joyful faces; but the appearance of a stranger blunted many a gibe which had been prepared on Hobbie's lack of success in the deer-stalking. There was a little bustle among three handsome young women, each endeavouring to devolve upon another the task of ushering the stranger into the apartment, while probably all were anxious to escape for the purpose of making some little personal arrangements, before presenting themselves to a young gentleman in a dishabille only intended for their brother.

Hobbie, in the meanwhile, bestowing some hearty and general abuse upon them all (for Grace was not of the party), snatched the candle from the hand of one of the rustic coquettes, as she stood playing pretty with it in her hand, and ushered his guest into the family parlour, or rather hall; for the place having been a house of defence in former times, the sitting apartment was a vaulted and paved room, damp and dismal enough compared with the lodgings of the yeomanry of our days, but which, when well lighted up with a large sparkling fire of turf and bog-wood, seemed to Earnscliff a most comfortable exchange for the darkness and bleak blast of the hill. Kindly and repeatedly was he welcomed by the venerable old dame, the mistress of the family, who, dressed in her coif and pinners, her close and decent gown of homespun wool, but with a large gold necklace and ear-rings, looked, what she really was, the lady as well as the farmer's wife, while, seated in her chair of wicker, by the corner of the great chimney, she directed the evening occupations of the young women, and of two or three stout serving wenches, who sate plying their distaffs behind the backs of their young mistresses.

As soon as Earnscliff had been duly welcomed, and hasty orders issued for some addition to the evening meal, his grand-dame and sisters opened their battery upon Hobbie Elliot for his lack of success against the deer.

"Jenny needna have kept up her kitchen-fire for a' that Hobbie has brought hame," said one sister.

"Troth no, lass," said another; "the gathering peat, if it was weel blawn, wad dress a' our Hobbie's venison." [The gathering peat is the piece of turf left to treasure up the secret seeds of fire, without any generous consumption of fuel; in a word, to keep the fire alive.]

"Ay, or the low of the candle, if the wind wad let it hide steady," said a third; "if I were him, I would bring hame a black craw, rather than come back three times without a buck's horn to blaw on."

Hobbie turned from the one to the other, regarding them alternately with a frown on his brow, the augury of which was confuted by the good-humoured laugh on the lower part of his countenance. He then strove to propitiate them, by mentioning the intended present of his companion.

"In my young days," said the old lady, "a man wad hae been ashamed to come back frae the hill without a buck hanging on each side o' his horse, like a cadger carrying calves."

"I wish they had left some for us then, grannie," retorted Hobbie; "they've cleared the country o' them, thae auld friends o' yours, I'm thinking."

"We see other folk can find game, though you cannot, Hobbie," said the eldest sister, glancing a look at young Earnscliff.

"Weel, weel, woman, hasna every dog his day, begging Earnscliff's pardon for the auld saying--Mayna I hae his luck, and he mine, another time?--It's a braw thing for a man to be out a' day, and frighted--na, I winna say that neither but mistrysted wi' bogles in the hame-coming, an' then to hae to flyte wi' a wheen women that hae been doing naething a' the live-lang day, but whirling a bit stick, wi' a thread trailing at it, or boring at a clout."

"Frighted wi' bogles!" exclaimed the females, one and all,--for great was the regard then paid, and perhaps still paid, in these glens, to all such fantasies.

"I did not say frighted, now--I only said mis-set wi' the thing --And there was but ae bogle, neither--Earnscliff, ye saw it; as weel as I did?"

And he proceeded, without very much exaggeration, to detail, in his own way, the meeting they had with the mysterious being at Mucklestane-Moor, concluding, he could not conjecture what on earth it could be, unless it was either the Enemy himsell, or some of the auld Peghts that held the country lang syne.

"Auld Peght!" exclaimed the grand-dame; "na, na--bless thee frae scathe, my bairn, it's been nae Peght that--it's been the Brown Man of the Moors! O weary fa' thae evil days!--what can evil beings be coming for to distract a poor country, now it's peacefully settled, and living in love and law--O weary on him! he ne'er brought gude to these lands or the indwellers. My father aften tauld me he was seen in the year o' the bloody fight at Marston-Moor, and then again in Montrose's troubles, and again before the rout o' Dunbar, and, in my ain time, he was seen about the time o' Bothwell-Brigg, and they said the second-sighted Laird of Benarbuck had a communing wi' him some time afore Argyle's landing, but that I cannot speak to sae preceesely--it was far in the west.--O, bairns, he's never permitted but in an ill time, sae mind ilka ane o' ye to draw to Him that can help in the day of trouble."

Earnscliff now interposed, and expressed his firm conviction that the person they had seen was some poor maniac, and had no commission from the invisible world to announce either war or evil. But his opinion found a very cold audience, and all joined to deprecate his purpose of returning to the spot the next day.

"O, my bonny bairn," said the old dame (for, in the kindness of her heart, she extended her parental style to all in whom she was interested)---"You should beware mair than other folk--there's been a heavy breach made in your house wi' your father's bloodshed, and wi' law-pleas, and losses sinsyne;--and you are the flower of the flock, and the lad that will build up the auld bigging again (if it be His will) to be an honour to the country, and a safeguard to those that dwell in it--you, before others, are called upon to put yoursell in no rash adventures--for yours was aye ower venturesome a race, and muckle harm they have got by it."

"But I am sure, my good friend, you would not have me be afraid of going to an open moor in broad daylight?"

"I dinna ken," said the good old dame; "I wad never bid son or friend o' mine haud their hand back in a gude cause, whether it were a friend's or their ain--that should be by nae bidding of mine, or of ony body that's come of a gentle kindred--But it winna gang out of a grey head like mine, that to gang to seek for evil that's no fashing wi' you, is clean against law and Scripture."

Earnscliff resigned an argument which he saw no prospect of maintaining with good effect, and the entrance of supper broke off the conversation. Miss Grace had by this time made her appearance, and Hobbie, not without a conscious glance at Earnscliff, placed himself by her side. Mirth and lively conversation, in which the old lady of the house took the good- humoured share which so well becomes old age, restored to the cheeks of the damsels the roses which their brother's tale of the apparition had chased away, and they danced and sung for an hour after supper as if there were no such things as goblins in the world.

CHAPTER IV.

I am Misanthropos, and hate mankind; For thy part, I do wish thou wert a dog, That I might love thee something. TIMON OF ATHENS

On the following morning, after breakfast, Earnscliff took leave of his hospitable friends, promising to return in time to partake of the venison, which had arrived from his house. Hobbie, who apparently took leave of him at the door of his habitation, slunk out, however, and joined him at the top of the hill.

"Ye'll be gaun yonder, Mr. Patrick; feind o' me will mistryst you for a' my mother says. I thought it best to slip out quietly though, in case she should mislippen something of what we're gaun to do--we maunna vex her at nae rate--it was amaist the last word my father said to me on his deathbed."

"By no means, Hobbie," said Earnscliff; "she well merits all your attention."

"Troth, for that matter, she would be as sair vexed amaist for you as for me. But d'ye really think there's nae presumption in venturing back yonder?--We hae nae special commission, ye ken."

"If I thought as you do, Hobbie," said the young gentleman, "I would not perhaps enquire farther into this business; but as I am of opinion that preternatural visitations are either ceased altogether, or become very rare in our days, I am unwilling to leave a matter uninvestigated which may concern the life of a poor distracted being."

"Aweel, aweel, if ye really think that," answered Hobbie doubtfully--"And it's for certain the very fairies--I mean the very good neighbours themsells (for they say folk suldna ca' them fairies) that used to be seen on every green knowe at e'en, are no half sae often visible in our days. I canna depone to having ever seen ane mysell, but, I ance heard ane whistle ahint me in the moss, as like a whaup [Curlew] as ae thing could be like anither. And mony ane my father saw when he used to come hame frae the fairs at e'en, wi' a drap drink in his head, honest man."

Earnscliff was somewhat entertained with the gradual declension of superstition from one generation to another which was inferred In this last observation; and they continued to reason on such subjects, until they came in sight of the upright stone which gave name to the moor.

"As I shall answer," says Hobbie, "yonder's the creature creeping about yet!--But it's daylight, and you have your gun, and I brought out my bit whinger--I think we may venture on him."

"By all manner of means," said Earnscliff; "but, in the name of wonder, what can he be doing there?"

"Biggin a dry-stane dyke, I think, wi' the grey geese, as they ca' thae great loose stanes--Odd, that passes a' thing I e'er heard tell of!"

As they approached nearer, Earnscliff could not help agreeing with his companion. The figure they had seen the night before seemed slowly and toilsomely labouring to pile the large stones one upon another, as if to form a small enclosure. Materials lay around him in great plenty, but the labour of carrying on the work was immense, from the size of most of the stones; and it seemed astonishing that he should have succeeded in moving several which he had already arranged for the foundation of his edifice. He was struggling to move a fragment of great size when the two young men came up, and was so intent upon executing his purpose, that he did not perceive them till they were close upon him. In straining and heaving at the stone, in order to place it according to his wish, he displayed a degree of strength which seemed utterly inconsistent with his size and apparent deformity. Indeed, to judge from the difficulties he had already surmounted, he must have been of Herculean powers; for some of the stones he had succeeded in raising apparently required two men's strength to have moved them. Hobbie's suspicions began to revive, on seeing the preternatural strength he exerted.

"I am amaist persuaded it's the ghaist of a stane-mason--see siccan band-statnes as he's laid i--An it be a man, after a', I wonder what he wad take by the rood to build a march dyke. There's ane sair wanted between Cringlehope and the Shaws.-- Honest man" (raising his voice), "ye make good firm wark there?"

The being whom he addressed raised his eyes with a ghastly stare, and, getting up from his stooping posture, stood before them in all his native and hideous deformity. His head was of uncommon size, covered with a fell of shaggy hair, partly grizzled with age; his eyebrows, shaggy and prominent, overhung a pair of small dark, piercing eyes, set far back in their sockets, that rolled with a portentous wildness, indicative of a partial insanity. The rest of his features were of the coarse, rough-hewn stamp, with which a painter would equip a giant in romance; to which was added the wild, irregular, and peculiar expression, so often seen in the countenances of those whose persons are deformed. His body, thick and square, like that of a man of middle size, was mounted upon two large feet; but nature seemed to have forgotten the legs and the thighs, or they were so very short as to be hidden by the dress which he wore. His arms were long and brawny, furnished with two muscular hands, and, where uncovered in the eagerness of his labour, were shagged with coarse black hair. It seemed as if nature had originally intended the separate parts of his body to be the members of a giant, but had afterwards capriciously assigned them to the person of a dwarf, so ill did the length of his arms and the iron strength of his frame correspond with the shortness of his stature. His clothing was a sort of coarse brown tunic, like a monk's frock, girt round him with a belt of seal-skin. On his head he had a cap made of badger's skin, or some other rough fur, which added considerably to the grotesque effect of his whole appearance, and overshadowed features, whose habitual expression seemed that of sullen malignant misanthropy.

This remarkable Dwarf gazed on the two youths in silence, with a dogged and irritated look, until Earnscliff, willing to soothe him into better temper, observed, "You are hard tasked, my friend; allow us to assist you."

Elliot and he accordingly placed the stone, by their joint efforts, upon the rising wall. The Dwarf watched them with the eye of a taskmaster, and testified, by peevish gestures, his impatience at the time which they took in adjusting the stone. He pointed to another-- they raised it also--to a third, to a fourth--they continued to humour him, though with some trouble, for he assigned them, as if intentionally, the heaviest fragments which lay near.

"And now, friend," said Elliot, as the unreasonable Dwarf indicated another stone larger than any they had moved, "Earnscliff may do as he likes; but be ye man or be ye waur, deil be in my fingers if I break my back wi' heaving thae stanes ony langer like a barrow-man, without getting sae muckle as thanks for my pains."

"Thanks!" exclaimed the Dwarf, with a motion expressive of the utmost contempt--"There--take them, and fatten upon them! Take them, and may they thrive with you as they have done with me--as they have done with every mortal worm that ever heard the word spoken by his fellow reptile! Hence--either labour or begone!"

"This is a fine reward we have, Earnscliff, for building a tabernacle for the devil, and prejudicing our ain souls into the bargain, for what we ken."

"Our presence," answered Earnscliff, "seems only to irritate his frenzy; we had better leave him, and send some one to provide him with food and necessaries."

They did so. The servant dispatched for this purpose found the Dwarf still labouring at his wall, but could not extract a word from him. The lad, infected with the superstitions of the country, did not long persist in an attempt to intrude questions or advice on so singular a figure, but having placed the articles which he had brought for his use on a stone at some distance, he left them at the misanthrope's disposal.

The Dwarf proceeded in his labours, day after day, with an assiduity so incredible as to appear almost supernatural. In one day he often seemed to have done the work of two men, and his building soon assumed the appearance of the walls of a hut, which, though very small, and constructed only of stones and turf, without any mortar, exhibited, from the unusual size of the stones employed, an appearance of solidity very uncommon for a cottage of such narrow dimensions and rude construction. Earnscliff; attentive to his motions, no sooner perceived to what they tended, than he sent down a number of spars of wood suitable for forming the roof, which he caused to be left in the neighbourhood of the spot, resolving next day to send workmen to put them up. But his purpose was anticipated, for in the evening, during the night, and early in the morning, the Dwarf had laboured so hard, and with such ingenuity, that he had nearly completed the adjustment of the rafters. His next labour was to cut rushes and thatch his dwelling, a task which he performed with singular dexterity.

As he seemed averse to receive any aid beyond the occasional assistance of a passenger, materials suitable to his purpose, and tools, were supplied to him, in the use of which he proved to be skilful. He constructed the door and window of his cot, he adjusted a rude bedstead, and a few shelves, and appeared to become somewhat soothed in his temper as his accommodations increased.

His next task was to form a strong enclosure, and to cultivate the land within it to the best of his power; until, by transporting mould, and working up what was upon the spot, he formed a patch of garden-ground. It must be naturally supposed, that, as above hinted, this solitary being received assistance occasionally from such travellers as crossed the moor by chance, as well as from several who went from curiosity to visit his works. It was, indeed, impossible to see a human creature, so unfitted, at first sight, for hard labour, toiling with such unremitting assiduity, without stopping a few minutes to aid him in his task; and, as no one of his occasional assistants was acquainted with the degree of help which the Dwarf had received from others, the celerity of his progress lost none of its marvels in their eyes. The strong and compact appearance of the cottage, formed in so very short a space, and by such a being, and the superior skill which he displayed in mechanics, and in other arts, gave suspicion to the surrounding neighbours. They insisted, that, if he was not a phantom,--an opinion which was now abandoned, since he plainly appeared a being of blood and bone with themselves,--yet he must be in close league with the invisible world, and have chosen that sequestered spot to carry on his communication with them undisturbed. They insisted, though in a different sense from the philosopher's application of the phrase, that he was never less alone than when alone; and that from the heights which commanded the moor at a distance, passengers often discovered a person at work along with this dweller of the desert, who regularly disappeared as soon as they approached closer to the cottage. Such a figure was also occasionally seen sitting beside him at the door, walking with him in the moor, or assisting him in fetching water from his fountain. Earnscliff explained this phenomenon by supposing it to be the Dwarf's shadow.

"Deil a shadow has he," replied Hobbie Elliot, who was a strenuous defender of the general opinion; "he's ower far in wi' the Auld Ane to have a shadow. Besides," he argued more logically, "wha ever heard of a shadow that cam between a body and the sun? and this thing, be it what it will, is thinner and taller than the body himsell, and has been seen to come between him and the sun mair than anes or twice either."

These suspicions, which, in any other part of the country, might have been attended with investigations a little inconvenient to the supposed wizard, were here only productive of respect and awe. The recluse being seemed somewhat gratified by the marks of timid veneration with which an occasional passenger approached his dwelling, the look of startled surprise with which he surveyed his person and his premises, and the hurried step with which he pressed his retreat as he passed the awful spot. The boldest only stopped to gratify their curiosity by a hasty glance at the walls of his cottage and garden, and to apologize for it by a courteous salutation, which the inmate sometimes deigned to return by a word or a nod. Earnscliff often passed that way, and seldom without enquiring after the solitary inmate, who seemed now to have arranged his establishment for life.

It was impossible to engage him in any conversation on his own personal affairs; nor was he communicative or accessible in talking on any other subject whatever, although he seemed to have considerably relented in the extreme ferocity of his misanthropy, or rather to be less frequently visited with the fits of derangement of which this was a symptom. No argument could prevail upon him to accept anything beyond the simplest necessaries, although much more was offered by Earnscliff out of charity, and by his more superstitious neighbours from other motives. The benefits of these last he repaid by advice, when consulted (as at length he slowly was) on their diseases, or those of their cattle. He often furnished them with medicines also, and seemed possessed, not only of such as were the produce of the country, but of foreign drugs. He gave these persons to understand, that his name was Elshender the Recluse; but his popular epithet soon came to be Canny Elshie, or the Wise Wight of Mucklestane-Moor. Some extended their queries beyond their bodily complaints, and requested advice upon other matters, which he delivered with an oracular shrewdness that greatly confirmed the opinion of his possessing preternatural skill. The querists usually left some offering upon a stone, at a distance from his dwelling; if it was money, or any article which did not suit him to accept, he either threw it away, or suffered it to remain where it was without making use of it. On all occasions his manners were rude and unsocial; and his words, in number, just sufficient to express his meaning as briefly as possible, and he shunned all communication that went a syllable beyond the matter in hand. When winter had passed away, and his garden began to afford him herbs and vegetables, he confined himself almost entirely to those articles of food. He accepted, notwithstanding, a pair of she-goats from Earnscliff, which fed on the moor, and supplied him with milk.

When Earnscliff found his gift had been received, he soon afterwards paid the hermit a visit. The old man was seated an a broad flat stone near his garden door, which was the seat of science he usually occupied when disposed to receive his patients or clients. The inside of his hut, and that of his garden, he kept as sacred from human intrusion as the natives of Otaheite do their Morai;--apparently he would have deemed it polluted by the step of any human being. When he shut himself up in his habitation, no entreaty could prevail upon him to make himself visible, or to give audience to any one whomsoever.

Earnscliff had been fishing in a small river at some distance. He had his rod in his hand, and his basket, filled with trout, at his shoulder. He sate down upon a stone nearly opposite to the Dwarf who, familiarized with his presence, took no farther notice of him than by elevating his huge mis-shapen head for the purpose of staring at him, and then again sinking it upon his bosom, as if in profound meditation. Earnscliff looked around him, and observed that the hermit had increased his accommodations by the construction of a shed for the reception of his goats.

You labour hard, Elshie," he said, willing to lead this singular being into conversation.

"Labour," re-echoed the Dwarf, "is the mildest evil of a lot so miserable as that of mankind; better to labour like me, than sport like you."

"I cannot defend the humanity of our ordinary rural sports, Elshie, and yet--"

"And yet," interrupted the Dwarf" they are better than your ordinary business; better to exercise idle and wanton cruelty on mute fishes than on your fellow-creatures. Yet why should I say so? Why should not the whole human herd butt, gore, and gorge upon each other, till all are extirpated but one huge and over- fed Behemoth, and he, when he had throttled and gnawed the bones of all his fellows--he, when his prey failed him, to be roaring whole days for lack of food, and, finally, to die, inch by inch, of famine--it were a consummation worthy of the race!"

"Your deeds are better, Elshie, than your words," answered Earnscliff; "you labour to preserve the race whom your misanthropy slanders."

"I do; but why?--Hearken. You are one on whom I look with the least loathing, and I care not, if, contrary to my wont, I waste a few words in compassion to your infatuated blindness. If I cannot send disease into families, and murrain among the herds, can I attain the same end so well as by prolonging the lives of those who can serve the purpose of destruction as effectually?-- If Alice of Bower had died in winter, would young Ruthwin have been slain for her love the last spring?--Who thought of penning their cattle beneath the tower when the Red Reiver of Westburnflat was deemed to be on his death-bed?--My draughts, my skill, recovered him. And, now, who dare leave his herd upon the lea without a watch, or go to bed without unchaining the sleuth- hound?"

"I own," answered Earnscliff; "you did little good to society by the last of these cures. But, to balance the evil, there is my friend Hobbie, honest Hobbie of the Heugh-foot, your skill relieved him last winter in a fever that might have cost him his life."

"Thus think the children of clay in their ignorance," said: the Dwarf, smiling maliciously, "and thus they speak in their folly. Have you marked the young cub of a wild cat that has been domesticated, how sportive, how playful, how gentle,--but trust him with your game, your lambs, your poultry, his inbred ferocity breaks forth; he gripes, tears, ravages, and devours."

"Such is the animal's instinct," answered Earnscliff; "but what has that to do with Hobbie?"

"It is his emblem--it is his picture," retorted the Recluse. "He is at present tame, quiet, and domesticated, for lack of opportunity to exercise his inborn propensities; but let the trumpet of war sound-- let the young blood-hound snuff blood, he will be as ferocious as the wildest of his Border ancestors that ever fired a helpless peasant's abode. Can you deny, that even at present he often urges you to take bloody revenge for an injury received when you were a boy?"-- Earnscliff started; the Recluse appeared not to observe his surprise, and proceeded--"The trumpet WILL blow, the young blood-hound WILL lap blood, and I will laugh and say, For this I have preserved thee!" He paused, and continued,--"Such are my cures;--their object, their purpose, perpetuating the mass of misery, and playing even in this desert my part in the general tragedy. Were YOU on your sick bed, I might, in compassion, send you a cup of poison."

"I am much obliged to you, Elshie, and certainly shall not fail to consult you, with so comfortable a hope from your assistance."

"Do not flatter yourself too far," replied the Hermit, "with the hope that I will positively yield to the frailty of pity. Why should I snatch a dupe, so well fitted to endure the miseries of life as you are, from the wretchedness which his own visions, and the villainy of the world, are preparing for him? Why should I play the compassionate Indian, and, knocking out the brains of the captive with my tomahawk, at once spoil the three days' amusement of my kindred tribe, at the very moment when the brands were lighted, the pincers heated, the cauldrons boiling, the knives sharpened, to tear, scorch, seethe, and scarify the intended victim?"

"A dreadful picture you present to me of life, Elshie; but I am not daunted by it," returned Earnscliff. "We are sent here, in one sense, to bear and to suffer; but, in another, to do and to enjoy. The active day has its evening of repose; even patient sufferance has its alleviations, where there is a consolatory sense of duty discharged."

"I spurn at the slavish and bestial doctrine," said the Dwarf, his eyes kindling with insane fury,--"I spurn at it, as worthy only of the beasts that perish; but I will waste no more words with you."

He rose hastily; but, ere he withdrew into the hut, he added, with great vehemence, "Yet, lest you still think my apparent benefits to mankind flow from the stupid and servile source, called love of our fellow-creatures, know, that were there a man who had annihilated my soul's dearest hope--who had torn my heart to mammocks, and seared mp brain till it glowed like a volcano, and were that man's fortune and life in my power as completely as this frail potsherd" (he snatched up an earthen cup which stood beside him), "I would not dash him into atoms thus"--(he flung the vessel with fury against the wall),--"No!" (he spoke more composedly, but with the utmost bitterness), "I would pamper him with wealth and power to inflame his evil passions, and to fulfil his evil designs; he should lack no means of vice and villainy; he should be the centre of a whirlpool that itself should know neither rest nor peace, but boil with unceasing fury, while it wrecked every goodly ship that approached its limits! he should be an earthquake capable of shaking the very land in which he dwelt, and rendering all its inhabitants friendless, outcast, and miserable--as I am!"

The wretched being rushed into his hut as he uttered these last words, shutting the door with furious violence, and rapidly drawing two bolts, one after another, as if to exclude the intrusion of any one of that hated race, who had thus lashed his soul to frenzy. Earnscliff left the moor with mingled sensations of pity and horror, pondering what strange and melancholy cause could have reduced to so miserable a state of mind, a man whose language argued him to be of rank and education much superior to the vulgar. He was also surprised to see how much particular information a person who had lived in that country so short a time, and in so recluse a manner, had been able to collect respecting the dispositions and private affairs of the inhabitants.

"It is no wonder," he said to himself, "that with such extent of information, such a mode of life, so uncouth a figure, and sentiments so virulently misanthropic, this unfortunate should be regarded by the vulgar as in league with the Enemy of Mankind."

CHAPTER V.

The bleakest rock upon the loneliest heath Feels, in its barrenness, some touch of spring; And, in the April dew, or beam of May, Its moss and lichen freshen and revive; And thus the heart, most sear'd to human pleasure, Melts at the tear, joys in the smile, of woman.
BEAUMONT

As the season advanced, the weather became more genial, and the Recluse was more frequently found occupying the broad flat stone in the front of his mansion. As he sate there one day, about the hour of noon, a party of gentlemen and ladies, well mounted, and numerously attended, swept across the heath at some distance from his dwelling. Dogs, hawks, and led-horses swelled the retinue, and the air resounded at intervals with the cheer of the hunters, and the sound of horns blown by the attendants. The Recluse was about to retire into his mansion at the sight of a train so joyous, when three young ladies, with their attendants, who had made a circuit, and detached themselves from their party, in order to gratify their curiosity by a sight of the Wise Wight of Mucklestane-Moor, came suddenly up, ere he could effect his purpose. The first shrieked, and put her hands before her eyes, at sight of an object so unusually deformed. The second, with a hysterical giggle, which she intended should disguise her terrors, asked the Recluse, whether he could tell their fortune. The third, who was best mounted, best dressed, and incomparably the best-looking of the three, advanced, as if to cover the incivility of her companions.

"We have lost the right path that leads through these morasses, and our party have gone forward without us," said the young lady. "Seeing you, father, at the door of your house, we have turned this way to--"

"Hush!" interrupted the Dwarf; "so young, and already so artful? You came--you know you came, to exult in the consciousness of your own youth, wealth, and beauty, by contrasting them with age, poverty, and deformity. It is a fit employment for the daughter of your father; but O how unlike the child of your mother!"

"Did you, then, know my parents, and do you know me?"

"Yes; this is the first time you have crossed my waking eyes, but I have seen you in my dreams."

45

"Your dreams?"

"Ay, Isabel Vere. What hast thou, or thine, to do with my waking thoughts?"

"Your waking thoughts, sir," said the second of Miss Vere's companions, with a sort of mock gravity, "are fixed, doubtless, upon wisdom; folly can only intrude on your sleeping moments."

"Over thine," retorted the Dwarf, more splenetically than became a philosopher or hermit, "folly exercises an unlimited empire, asleep or awake."

"Lord bless us!" said the lady, "he's a prophet, sure enough."

"As surely," continued the Recluse," as thou art a woman.--A woman!--I should have said a lady--a fine lady. You asked me to tell your fortune--it is a simple one; an endless chase through life after follies not worth catching, and, when caught, successively thrown away--a chase, pursued from the days of tottering infancy to those of old age upon his crutches. Toys and merry-makings in childhood--love and its absurdities in youth--spadille and basto in age, shall succeed each other as objects of pursuit--flowers and butterflies in spring-- butterflies and thistle-down in summer--withered leaves in autumn and winter--all pursued, all caught, all flung aside. --Stand apart; your fortune is said."

"All CAUGHT, however," retorted the laughing fair one, who was a cousin of Miss Vere's; "that's something, Nancy," she continued, turning to the timid damsel who had first approached the Dwarf; "will you ask your fortune?"

"Not for worlds," said she, drawing back; "I have heard enough of yours."

"Well, then," said Miss Ilderton, offering money to the Dwarf, "I'll pay for mine, as if it were spoken by an oracle to a princess."

"Truth," said the Soothsayer, "can neither be bought nor sold;" and he pushed back her proffered offering with morose disdain.

"Well, then," said the lady, "I'll keep my money, Mr. Elshender, to assist me in the chase I am to pursue."

"You will need it," replied the cynic; "without it, few pursue successfully, and fewer are themselves pursued.--Stop!" he said to Miss Vere, as her companions moved off, "With you I have more to say. You have what your companions would wish to have, or be thought to have,--beauty, wealth, station, accomplishments."

"Forgive my following my companions, father; I am proof both to flattery and fortune-telling."

"Stay," continued the Dwarf, with his hand on her horse's rein, "I am no common soothsayer, and I am no flatterer. All the advantages I have detailed, all and each of them have their corresponding evils-- unsuccessful love, crossed affections, the gloom of a convent, or an odious alliance. I, who wish ill to all mankind, cannot wish more evil to you, so much is your course of life crossed by it."

"And if it be, father, let me enjoy the readiest solace of adversity while prosperity is in my power. You are old; you are poor; your habitation is far from human aid, were you ill, or in want; your situation, in many respects, exposes you to the suspicions of the vulgar, which are too apt to break out into actions of brutality. Let me think I have mended the lot of one human being! Accept of such assistance as I have power to offer; do this for my sake, if not for your own, that when these evils arise, which you prophesy perhaps too truly, I may not have to reflect, that the hours of my happier time have been passed altogether in vain."

The old man answered with a broken voice, and almost without addressing himself to the young lady,--

"Yes, 'tis thus thou shouldst think--'tis thus thou shouldst speak, if ever human speech and thought kept touch with each other! They do not--they do not--Alas! they cannot. And yet-- wait here an instant-- stir not till my return." He went to his little garden, and returned with a half-blown rose. "Thou hast made me shed a tear, the first which has wet my eyelids for many a year; for that good deed receive this token of gratitude. It is but a common rose; preserve it, however, and do not part with it. Come to me in your hour of adversity. Show me that rose, or but one leaf of it, were it withered as my heart is--if it should be in my fiercest and wildest movements of rage against a hateful world, still it will recall gentler thoughts to my bosom, and perhaps afford happier prospects to thine. But no message," he exclaimed, rising into his usual mood of misanthropy,-- "no message--no go-between! Come thyself; and the heart and the doors that are shut against every other earthly being, shall open to thee and to thy sorrows. And now pass on."

He let go the bridle-rein, and the young lady rode on, after expressing her thanks to this singular being, as well as her surprise at the extraordinary nature of his address would permit, often turning back to look at the Dwarf, who still remained at the door of his habitation, and watched her progress over the moor towards her father's castle of Ellieslaw, until the brow of the hill hid the party from his sight.

The ladies, meantime, jested with Miss Vere on the strange interview they had just had with the far-famed wizard of the Moor. "Isabella has all the luck at home and abroad! Her hawk strikes down the black-cock; her eyes wound the gallant; no chance for her poor companions and kinswomen; even the conjuror cannot escape the force of her charms. You should, in compassion, cease to be such an engrosser, my dear Isabel, or at least set up shop, and sell off all the goods you do not mean to keep for your own use."

"You shall have them all," replied Miss Vere, "and the conjuror to boot, at a very easy rate."

"No! Nancy shall have the conjuror," said Miss Ilderton, "to supply deficiencies; she's not quite a witch herself, you know."

"Lord, sister," answered the younger Miss Ilderton, "what could I do with so frightful a monster? I kept my eyes shut, after once glancing at him; and, I protest, I thought I saw him still, though I winked as close as ever I could."

"That's a pity," said her sister; "ever while you live, Nancy, choose an admirer whose faults can be hid by winking at them.-- Well, then, I must take him myself, I suppose, and put him into mamma's Japan cabinet, in order to show that Scotland can produce a specimen of mortal clay moulded into a form ten thousand times uglier than the imaginations of Canton and Pekin, fertile as they are in monsters, have immortalized in porcelain."

"There is something," said Miss Vere, "so melancholy in the situation of this poor man, that I cannot enter into your mirth, Lucy, so readily as usual. If he has no resources, how is he to exist in this waste country, living, as he does, at such a distance from mankind? and if he has the means of securing occasional assistance, will not the very suspicion that he is possessed of them, expose him to plunder and assassination by some of our unsettled neighbours?"

"But you forget that they say he is a warlock," said Nancy Ilderton.

"And, if his magic diabolical should fail him," rejoined her sister, "I would have him trust to his magic natural, and thrust his enormous head, and most preternatural visage, out at his door or window, full in view of the assailants. The boldest robber that ever rode would hardly bide a second glance of him. Well, I wish I had the use of that Gorgon head of his for only one half hour."

"For what purpose, Lucy?" said Miss Vere.

"O! I would frighten out of the castle that dark, stiff, and stately Sir Frederick Langley, that is so great a favourite with your father, and so little a favourite of yours. I protest I shall be obliged to the Wizard as long as I live, if it were only for the half hour's relief from that man's company which we have gained by deviating from the party to visit Elshie."

"What would you say, then," said Miss Vere, in a low tone, so as not to be heard by the younger sister, who rode before them, the narrow path not admitting of their moving all three abreast,--" What would you say, my dearest Lucy, if it were proposed to you to endure his company for life?"

"Say? I would say, NO, NO, NO, three times, each louder than another, till they should hear me at Carlisle."

"And Sir Frederick would say then, nineteen nay-says are half a grant."

"That," replied Miss Lucy, "depends entirely on the manner in which the nay-says are said. Mine should have not one grain of concession in them, I promise you."

"But if your father," said Miss Vere, "were to say,--Thus do, or --"

"I would stand to the consequences of his OR, were he the most cruel father that ever was recorded in romance,. to fill up the alternative."

"And what if he threatened you with a catholic aunt, an abbess, and a cloister?"

"Then," said Miss Ilderton, "I would threaten him with a protestant son-in-law, and be glad of an opportunity to disobey him for conscience' sake. And now that Nancy is out of hearing, let me really say, I think you would be excusable before God and man for resisting this preposterous match by every means in your power. A proud, dark, ambitious man; a caballer against the state; infamous for his avarice and severity; a bad son, a bad brother, unkind and ungenerous to all his relatives--Isabel, I would die rather than have him."

"Don't let my father hear you give me such advice," said Miss Vere, "or adieu, my dear Lucy, to Ellieslaw Castle."

"And adieu to Ellieslaw Castle, with all my heart," said her friend, "if I once saw you fairly out of it, and settled under some kinder protector than he whom nature has given you. O, if my poor father had been in his former health, how gladly would he have received and sheltered you, till this ridiculous and cruel persecution were blown over!"

"Would to God it had been so, my dear Lucy!" answered Isabella; "but I fear, that, in your father's weak state of health, he would be altogether unable to protect me against the means which would be immediately used for reclaiming the poor fugitive."

"I fear so indeed," replied Miss Ilderton; "but we will consider and devise something. Now that your father and his guests seem so deeply engaged in some mysterious plot, to judge from the passing and returning of messages, from the strange faces which appear and disappear without being announced by their names, from the collecting and cleaning of arms, and the anxious gloom and bustle which seem to agitate every male in the castle, it may not be impossible for us (always in case matters be driven to extremity) to shape out some little supplemental conspiracy of our own. I hope the gentlemen have not kept all the policy to themselves; and there is one associate that I would gladly admit to our counsel."

"Not Nancy?"

"O, no!" said Miss Ilderton; "Nancy, though an excellent good girl, and fondly attached to you, would make a dull conspirator --as dull as Renault and all the other subordinate plotters in VENICE PRESERVED. No; this is a Jaffier, or Pierre, if you like the character better; and yet though I know I shall please you, I am afraid to mention his name to you, lest I vex you at the same time. Can you not guess? Something about an eagle and a rock-- it does not begin with eagle in English, but something very like it in Scotch."

"You cannot mean young Earnscliff, Lucy?" said Miss Vere, blushing deeply.

"And whom else should I mean" said Lucy. "Jaffiers and Pierres are very scarce in this country, I take it, though one could find Renaults and Bedamars enow."

"How call you talk so wildly, Lucy? Your plays and romances have positively turned your brain. You know, that, independent of my father's consent, without which I never will marry any one, and which, in the case you point at, would never be granted; independent, too, of our knowing nothing of young Earnscliff's inclinations, but by your own vivid conjectures and fancies-- besides all this, there is the fatal brawl!"

"When his father was killed?" said Lucy. "But that was very long ago; and I hope we have outlived the time of bloody feud, when a quarrel was carried down between two families from father to son, like a Spanish game at chess, and a murder or two committed in every generation, just to keep the matter from going to sleep. We do with our quarrels nowadays as with our clothes; cut them out for ourselves, and wear them out in our own day, and should no more think of resenting our fathers' feuds, than of wearing their slashed doublets and trunk-hose."

"You treat this far too lightly, Lucy," answered Miss Vere.

"Not a bit, my dear Isabella," said Lucy. "Consider, your father, though present in the unhappy affray, is never supposed to have struck the fatal blow; besides, in former times, in case of mutual slaughter between clans, subsequent alliances were so far from being excluded, that the hand of a daughter or a sister was the most frequent gage of reconciliation. You laugh at my skill in romance; but, I assure you, should your history be written, like that of many a less distressed and less deserving heroine, the well-judging reader would set you down for the lady and the love of Earnscliff; from the very obstacle which you suppose so insurmountable."

"But these are not the days of romance, but of sad reality, for there stands the castle of Ellieslaw."

"And there stands Sir Frederick Langley at the gate, waiting to assist the ladies from their palfreys. I would as lief touch a toad; I will disappoint him, and take old Horsington the groom for my master of the horse."

So saying, the lively young lady switched her palfrey forward, and passing Sir Frederick with a familiar nod as he stood ready to take her horse's rein, she cantered on, and jumped into the arms of the old groom. Fain would Isabella have done the same had she dared; but her father stood near, displeasure already darkening on a countenance peculiarly qualified to express the harsher passions, and she was compelled to receive the unwelcome assiduities of her detested suitor.

CHAPTER VI.

Let not us that are squires of the night's body be called thieves of the day's booty; let us be Diana's foresters, gentlemen of the shade, minions of the moon. HENRY THE FOURTH, PART I.

The Solitary had consumed the remainder of that day in which he had the interview with the young ladies, within the precincts of his garden. Evening again found him seated on his favourite stone. The sun setting red, and among seas of rolling clouds, threw a gloomy lustre over the moor, and gave a deeper purple to the broad outline of heathy mountains which surrounded this desolate spot. The Dwarf sate watching the clouds as they lowered above each other in masses of conglomerated vapours, and, as a strong lurid beam of the sinking luminary darted full on his solitary and uncouth figure, he might well have seemed the demon of the storm which was gathering, or some gnome summoned forth from the recesses of the earth by the subterranean signals of its approach. As he sate thus, with his dark eye turned towards the scowling and blackening heaven, a horseman rode rapidly up to him, and stopping, as if to let his horse breathe for an instant, made a sort of obeisance to the anchoret, with an air betwixt effrontery and embarrassment.

The figure of the rider was thin, tall, and slender, but remarkably athletic, bony, and sinewy; like one who had all his life followed those violent exercises which prevent the human form from increasing in bulk, while they harden and confirm by habit its muscular powers. His face, sharp-featured, sun-burnt, and freckled, had a sinister expression of violence, impudence, and cunning, each of which seemed alternately to predominate over the others. Sandy-coloured hair, and reddish eyebrows, from under which looked forth his sharp grey eyes, completed the inauspicious outline of the horseman's physiognomy. He had pistols in his holsters, and another pair peeped from his belt, though he had taken some pains to conceal them by buttoning his doublet. He wore a rusted steel head piece; a buff jacket of rather an antique cast; gloves, of which that for the right hand was covered with small scales of iron, like an ancient gauntlet; and a long broadsword completed his equipage.

"So," said the Dwarf," rapine and murder once more on horseback."

"On horseback?" said the bandit; "ay, ay, Elshie, your leech- craft has set me on the bonny bay again."

"And all those promises of amendment which you made during your illness forgotten?" continued Elshender.

"All clear away, with the water-saps and panada," returned the unabashed convalescent. "Ye ken, Elshie, for they say ye are weel acquent wi' the gentleman,

"When the devil was sick, the devil a monk would be, When the devil was well, the devil a monk was he."

"Thou say'st true," said the Solitary; "as well divide a wolf from his appetite for carnage, or a raven from her scent of slaughter, as thee from thy accursed propensities."

"Why, what would you have me to do? It's born with me--lies in my very blude and bane. Why, man, the lads of Westburnflat, for ten lang descents, have been reivers and lifters. They have all drunk hard, lived high, taking deep revenge for light offence, and never wanted gear for the winning."

"Right; and thou art as thorough-bred a wolf," said the Dwarf, "as ever leapt a lamb-fold at night. On what hell's errand art thou bound now?"

"Can your skill not guess?"

"Thus far I know," said the Dwarf, "that thy purpose is bad, thy deed will be worse,, and the issue worst of all."

"And you like me the better for it, Father Elshie, eh?" said Westburnflat; "you always said you did."

"I have cause to like all," answered the Solitary, "that are scourges to their fellow-creatures, and thou art a bloody one."

"No--I say not guilty to that--lever bluidy unless there's resistance, and that sets a man's bristles up, ye ken. And this is nae great matter, after a'; just to cut the comb of a young cock that has been crawing a little ower crousely."

"Not young Earnscliff?" said the Solitary, with some emotion.

"No; not young Earnscliff--not young Earnscliff YET; but his time may come, if he will not take warning, and get him back to the burrow-town that he's fit for, and no keep skelping about here, destroying the few deer that are left in the country, and pretending to act as a magistrate, and writing letters to the great folk at Auld Reekie, about the disturbed state of the land. Let him take care o' himsell."

"Then it must be Hobbie of the Heugh-foot," said Elshie. "What harm has the lad done you?"

"Harm! nae great harm; but I hear he says I staid away from the Ba'spiel on Fastern's E'en, for fear of him; and it was only for fear of the Country Keeper, for there was a warrant against me. I'll stand Hobbie's feud, and a' his clan's. But it's not so much for that, as to gie him a lesson not to let his tongue gallop ower freely about his betters. I trow he will hae lost the best pen-feather o' his wing before to-morrow morning.-- Farewell, Elshie; there's some canny boys waiting for me down amang the shaws, owerby; I will see you as I come back, and bring ye a blithe tale in return for your leech-craft."

Ere the Dwarf could collect himself to reply, the Reiver of Westburnflat set spurs to his horse. The animal, starting at one of the stones which lay scattered about, flew from the path. The rider exercised his spurs without moderation or mercy. The horse became furious, reared, kicked, plunged, and bolted like a deer, with all his four feet off the ground at once. It was in vain; the unrelenting rider sate as if he had been a part of the horse which he bestrode; and, after a short but furious contest, compelled the subdued animal to proceed upon the path at a rate which soon carried him out of sight of the Solitary.

"That villain," exclaimed the Dwarf,--"that cool-blooded, hardened, unrelenting ruffian,--that wretch, whose every thought is infected with crimes,--has thewes and sinews, limbs, strength, and activity enough, to compel a nobler animal than himself to carry him to the place where he is to perpetrate his wickedness; while I, had I the weakness to wish to put his wretched victim on his guard, and to save the helpless family, would see my good intentions frustrated by the decrepitude which chains me to the spot.--Why should I wish it were otherwise? What have my screech-owl voice, my hideous form, and my mis-shapen features, to do with the fairer workmanship of nature? Do not men receive even my benefits with shrinking horror and ill-suppressed disgust? And why should I interest myself in a race which accounts me a prodigy and an outcast, and which has treated me as such? No; by all the ingratitude which I have reaped-- by all the wrongs which I have sustained--by my imprisonment, my stripes, my chains, I will wrestle down my feelings of rebellious humanity! I will not be the fool I have been, to swerve from my principles whenever there was an appeal, forsooth, to my feelings; as if I, towards whom none show sympathy, ought to have sympathy with any one. Let Destiny drive forth her scythed car through the overwhelmed and trembling mass of humanity! Shall I be the idiot to throw this decrepit form, this mis-shapen lump of mortality, under her wheels, that the Dwarf, the Wizard, the Hunchback, may save from destruction some fair form or some active frame, and all the world clap their hands at the exchange? No, never!--And yet this Elliot--this Hobbie, so young and gallant, so frank, so --I will think of it no longer. I cannot aid him if I would, and I am resolved--firmly resolved, that I would not aid him, if a wish were the pledge of his safety!"

Having thus ended his soliloquy, he retreated into his hut for shelter from the storm which was fast approaching, and now began to burst in large and heavy drops of rain. The last rays of the sun now disappeared entirely, and two or three claps of distant thunder followed each other at brief intervals, echoing and re-echoing among the range of heathy fells like the sound of a distant engagement.

CHAPTER VII.

Proud bird of the mountain, thy plume shall be torn!-- . . . . Return to
thy dwelling; all lonely, return; For the blackness of ashes shall mark
where it stood, And a wild mother scream o'er her famishing brood.
CAMPBELL.

The night continued sullen and stormy; but morning rose as if
refreshed by the rains. Even the Mucklestane-Moor, with its broad
bleak swells of barren grounds, interspersed with marshy pools of
water, seemed to smile under the serene influence of the sky, just as
good-humour can spread a certain inexpressible charm over the
plainest human countenance. The heath was in its thickest and
deepest bloom. The bees, which the Solitary had added to his rural
establishment, were abroad and on the wing, and filled the air with
the murmurs of their industry. As the old man crept out of his little
hut, his two she-goats came to meet him, and licked his hands in
gratitude for the vegetables with which he supplied them from his
garden. "You, at least," he said--"you, at least, see no differences in
form which can alter your feelings to a benefactor--to you, the finest
shape that ever statuary moulded would be an object of indifference
or of alarm, should it present itself instead of the mis-shapen trunk
to whose services you are accustomed. While I was in the world, did
I ever meet with such a return of gratitude? No; the domestic whom
I had bred from infancy made mouths at me as he stood behind my
chair; the friend whom I had supported with my fortune, and for
whose sake I had even stained--(he stopped with a strong convulsive
shudder), even he thought me more fit for the society of lunatics--for
their disgraceful restraints--for their cruel privations, than for
communication with the rest of humanity. Hubert alone--and Hubert
too will one day abandon me. All are of a piece, one mass of
wickedness, selfishness, and ingratitude-- wretches, who sin even in
their devotions; and of such hardness of heart, that they do not,
without hypocrisy, even thank the Deity himself for his warm sun
and pure air."

As he was plunged in these gloomy soliloquies, he heard the tramp
of a horse on the other side of his enclosure, and a strong clear bass
voice singing with the liveliness inspired by a light heart,

Canny Hobbie Elliot, canny Hobbie now, Canny Hobbie Elliot, I'se
gang alang wi' you.

At the same moment, a large deer greyhound sprung over the hermit's fence. It is well known to the sportsmen in these wilds, that the appearance and scent of the goat so much resemble those of their usual objects of chase, that the best-broke greyhounds will sometimes fly upon them. The dog in question instantly pulled down and throttled one of the hermit's she- goats, while Hobbie Elliot, who came up, and jumped from his horse for the purpose, was unable to extricate the harmless animal from the fangs of his attendant until it was expiring. The Dwarf eyed, for a few moments, the convulsive starts of his dying favourite, until the poor goat stretched out her limbs with the twitches and shivering fit of the last agony. He then started into an access of frenzy, and unsheathing a long sharp knife, or dagger, which he wore under his coat, he was about to launch it at the dog, when Hobbie, perceiving his purpose, interposed, and caught hold of his hand, exclaiming, "Let a be the hound, man--let a be the hound!--Na, na, Killbuck maunna be guided that gate, neither."

The Dwarf turned his rage on the young farmer; and, by a sudden effort, far more powerful than Hobbie expected from such a person, freed his wrist from his grasp, and offered the dagger at his heart. All this was done in the twinkling of an eye, and the incensed Recluse might have completed his vengeance by plunging the weapon in Elliot's bosom, had he not been checked by an internal impulse which made him hurl the knife to a distance.

"No," he exclaimed, as he thus voluntarily deprived himself of the means of gratifying his rage; "not again--not again!"

Hobbie retreated a step or two in great surprise, discomposure, and disdain, at having been placed in such danger by an object apparently so contemptible.

"The deil's in the body for strength and bitterness!" were the first words that escaped him, which he followed up with an apology for the accident that had given rise to their disagreement. "I am no justifying Killbuck a'thegither neither, and I am sure it is as vexing to me as to you, Elshie, that the mischance should hae happened; but I'll send you twa goats and twa fat gimmers, man, to make a' straight again. A wise man like you shouldna bear malice against a poor dumb thing; ye see that a goat's like first-cousin to a deer, sae he acted but according to his nature after a'. Had it been a pet-lamb, there wad hae been mair to be said. Ye suld keep sheep, Elshie, and no goats, where there's sae mony deerhounds about--but I'll send ye baith."

"Wretch!" said the Hermit, "your cruelty has destroyed one of the only creatures in existence that would look on me with kindness!"

"Dear Elshie," answered Hobbie, "I'm wae ye suld hae cause to say sae; I'm sure it wasna wi' my will. And yet, it's true, I should hae minded your goats, and coupled up the dogs. I'm sure I would rather they had worried the primest wether in my faulds.--Come, man, forget and forgie. I'm e'en as vexed as ye can be--But I am a bridegroom, ye see, and that puts a' things out o' my head, I think. There's the marriage-dinner, or gude part o't, that my twa brithers are bringing on a sled round by the Riders' Slack, three goodly bucks as ever ran on Dallomlea, as the sang says; they couldna come the straight road for the saft grund. I wad send ye a bit venison, but ye wadna take it weel maybe, for Killbuck catched it."

During this long speech, in which the good-natured Borderer endeavoured to propitiate the offended Dwarf by every argument he could think of, he heard him with his eyes bent on the ground, as if in the deepest meditation, and at length broke forth-- "Nature?--yes! it is indeed in the usual beaten path of Nature. The strong gripe and throttle the weak; the rich depress and despoil the needy; the happy (those who are idiots enough to think themselves happy) insult the misery and diminish the consolation of the wretched.--Go hence, thou who hast contrived to give an additional pang to the most miserable of human beings --thou who hast deprived me of what I half considered as a source of comfort. Go hence, and enjoy the happiness prepared for thee at home!"

"Never stir," said Hobbie, "if I wadna take you wi' me, man, if ye wad but say it wad divert ye to be at the bridal on Monday. There will be a hundred strapping Elliots to ride the brouze--the like's no been seen sin' the days of auld Martin of the Preakin- tower--I wad send the sled for ye wi' a canny powny."

"Is it to me you propose once more to mix in the society of the common herd?" said the Recluse, with an air of deep disgust.

"Commons!" retorted Hobbie, "nae siccan commons neither; the Elliots hae been lang kend a gentle race."

"Hence! begone!" reiterated the Dwarf; "may the same evil luck attend thee that thou hast left behind with me! If I go not with you myself, see if you can escape what my attendants, Wrath and Misery, have brought to thy threshold before thee."

"I wish ye wadna speak that gate," said Hobbie. "Ye ken yoursell, Elshie, naebody judges you to be ower canny; now, I'll tell ye just ae word for a'--ye hae spoken as muckle as wussing ill to me and mine; now, if ony mischance happen to Grace, which God forbid, or to mysell; or to the poor dumb tyke; or if I be skaithed and injured in body, gudes, or gear, I'll no forget wha it is that it's owing to."

"Out, hind!" exclaimed the Dwarf; "home! home to your dwelling, and think on me when you find what has befallen there."

"Aweel, aweel," said Hobbie, mounting his horse, "it serves naething to strive wi' cripples,--they are aye cankered; but I'll just tell ye ae thing, neighbour, that if things be otherwise than weel wi' Grace Armstrong, I'se gie you a scouther if there be a tar-barrel in the five parishes."

So saying, he rode off; and Elshie, after looking at him with a scornful and indignant laugh, took spade and mattock, and occupied himself in digging a grave for his deceased favourite.

A low whistle, and the words, "Hisht, Elshie, hisht!" disturbed him in this melancholy occupation. He looked up, and the Red Reiver of Westburnflat was before him. Like Banquo's murderer, there was blood on his face, as well as upon the rowels of his spurs and the sides of his over-ridden horse.

"How now, ruffian!" demanded the Dwarf, "is thy job chared?"

"Ay, ay, doubt not that, Elshie," answered the freebooter; "When I ride, my foes may moan. They have had mair light than comfort at the Heugh-foot this morning; there's a toom byre and a wide, and a wail and a cry for the bonny bride."

"The bride?"

"Ay; Charlie Cheat-the-Woodie, as we ca' him, that's Charlie Foster of Tinning Beck, has promised to keep her in Cumberland till the blast blaw by. She saw me, and kend me in the splore, for the mask

60

fell frae my face for a blink. I am thinking it wad concern my safety if she were to come back here, for there's mony o' the Elliots, and they band weel thegither for right or wrang. Now, what I chiefly come to ask your rede in, is how to make her sure?"

"Wouldst thou murder her, then?"

"Umph! no, no; that I would not do, if I could help it. But they say they can whiles get folk cannily away to the plantations from some of the outports, and something to boot for them that brings a bonny wench. They're wanted beyond seas thae female cattle, and they're no that scarce here. But I think o' doing better for this lassie. There's a leddy, that, unless she be a' the better bairn, is to be sent to foreign parts whether she will or no; now, I think of sending Grace to wait on her--she's a bonny lassie. Hobbie will hae a merry morning when he comes hame, and misses baith bride and gear."

"Ay; and do you not pity him?" said the Recluse.

"Wad he pity me were I gaeing up the Castle hill at Jeddart? [The place of execution at that ancient burgh, where many of Westburnflat's profession have made their final exit.] And yet I rue something for the bit lassie; but he'll get anither, and little skaith dune--ane is as gude as anither. And now, you that like to hear o' splores, heard ye ever o' a better ane than I hae had this morning?"

"Air, ocean, and fire," said the Dwarf, speaking to himself, "the earthquake, the tempest, the volcano, are all mild and moderate, compared to the wrath of man. And what is this fellow, but one more skilled than others in executing the end of his existence? --Hear me, felon, go again where I before sent thee."

"To the Steward?"

"Ay; and tell him, Elshender the Recluse commands him to give thee gold. But, hear me, let the maiden be discharged free and uninjured; return her to her friends, and let her swear not to discover thy villainy."

"Swear" said Westburnflat; "but what if she break her aith? Women are not famous for keeping their plight. A wise man like you should ken that.--And uninjured--wha kens what may happen were she to be left lang at Tinning-Beck? Charlie Cheat-the-Woodie is a rough customer. But if the gold could be made up to twenty pieces, I think I could ensure her being wi' her friends within the twenty-four hours."

The Dwarf took his tablets from his pocket, marked a line on them, and tore out the leaf. "There," he said, giving the robber the leaf-- "But, mark me; thou knowest I am not to be fooled by thy treachery; if thou darest to disobey my directions, thy wretched life, be sure, shall answer it."

"I know," said the fellow, looking down, "that you have power on earth, however you came by it; you can do what nae other man can do, baith by physic and foresight; and the gold is shelled down when ye command, as fast as I have seen the ash-keys fall in a frosty morning in October. I will not disobey you."

"Begone, then, and relieve me of thy hateful presence."

The robber set spurs to his horse, and rode off without reply.

Hobbie Elliot had, in the meanwhile, pursued his journey rapidly, harassed by those oppressive and indistinct fears that all was not right, which men usually term a presentiment of misfortune. Ere he reached the top of the bank from which he could look down on his own habitation, he was met by his nurse, a person then of great consequence in all families in Scotland, whether of the higher or middling classes. The connexion between them and their foster-children was considered a tie far too dearly intimate to be broken; and it usually happened, in the course of years, that the nurse became a resident in the family of her foster-son, assisting in the domestic duties, and receiving all marks of attention and regard from the heads of the family. So soon as Hobbie recognised the figure of Annaple, in her red cloak and black hood, he could not help exclaiming to himself, "What ill luck can hae brought the auld nurse sae far frae hame, her that never stirs a gun-shot frae the door-stane for ordinar?--Hout, it will just be to get crane-berries, or whortle-berries, or some such stuff, out of the moss, to make the pies and tarts for the feast on Monday.--I cannot get the words of that cankered auld cripple deil's-buckie out o' my head--the least thing makes me dread some ill news.--O, Killbuck, man! were there nae deer and goats in the country besides, but ye behoved to gang and worry his creature, by a' other folk's?"

By this time Annaple, with a brow like a tragic volume, had hobbled towards him, and caught his horse by the bridle. The despair in her look was so evident as to deprive even him of the power of asking the cause. "O my bairn!" she cried, "gang na forward--gang na forward--it's a sight to kill onybody, let alane thee."

"In God's name, what's the matter?" said the astonished horseman, endeavouring to extricate his bridle from the grasp of the old woman; "for Heaven's sake, let me go and see what's the matter."

"Ohon! that I should have lived to see the day!--The steading's a' in a low, and the bonny stack-yard lying in the red ashes, and the gear a' driven away. But gang na forward ; it wad break your young heart, hinny, to see what my auld een hae seen this morning."

"And who has dared to do this? let go my bridle, Annaple--where is my grandmother--my sisters?--Where is Grace Armstrong?--God!-- the words of the warlock are knelling in my ears!"

He sprang from his horse to rid himself of Annaple's interruption, and, ascending the hill with great speed, soon came in view of the spectacle with which she had threatened him. It was indeed a heart-breaking sight. The habitation which he had left in its seclusion, beside the mountain-stream, surrounded with every evidence of rustic plenty, was now a wasted and blackened ruin. From amongst the shattered and sable walls the smoke continued to rise. The turf-stack, the barn-yard, the offices stocked with cattle, all the wealth of an upland cultivator of the period, of which poor Elliot possessed no common share, had been laid waste or carried off in a single night. He stood a moment motionless, and then exclaimed, "I am ruined-- ruined to the ground!--But curse on the warld's gear--Had it not been the week before the bridal--But I am nae babe, to sit down and greet about it. If I can but find Grace, and my grandmother, and my sisters weel, I can go to the wars in Flanders, as my gude-sire did, under the Bellenden banner, wi' auld Buccleuch. At ony rate, I will keep up a heart, or they will lose theirs a'thegither."

Manfully strode Hobbie down the hill, resolved to suppress his own despair, and administer consolation which he did not feel. The neighbouring inhabitants of the dell, particularly those of his own name, had already assembled. The younger part were in arms and clamorous for revenge, although they knew not upon whom; the elder were taking measures for the relief of the distressed family.

Annaple's cottage, which was situated down the brook, at some distance from the scene of mischief, had been hastily adapted for the temporary accommodation of the old lady and her daughters, with such articles as had been contributed by the neighbours, for very little was saved from the wreck.

"Are we to stand here a' day, sirs," exclaimed one tall young man, "and look at the burnt wa's of our kinsman's house? Every wreath of the reek is a blast of shame upon us! Let us to horse, and take the chase.--Who has the nearest bloodhound?"

"It's young Earnscliff," answered another; "and he's been on and away wi' six horse lang syne, to see if he can track them."

"Let us follow him then, and raise the country, and mak mair help as we ride, and then have at the Cumberland reivers! Take, burn, and slay--they that lie nearest us shall smart first."

"Whisht! haud your tongues, daft callants," said an old man, "ye dinna ken what ye speak about. What! wad ye raise war atween two pacificated countries?"

"And what signifies deaving us wi' tales about our fathers," retorted the young; man, "if we're to sit and see our friends' houses burnt ower their heads, and no put out hand to revenge them? Our fathers did not do that, I trow?"

"I am no saying onything against revenging Hobbie's wrang, puir chield; but we maun take the law wi' us in thae days, Simon," answered the more prudent elder.

"And besides," said another old man, "I dinna believe there's ane now living that kens the lawful mode of following a fray across the Border. Tam o' Whittram kend a' about it; but he died in the hard winter."

"Ay," said a third, "he was at the great gathering, when they chased as far as Thirlwall; it was the year after the fight of Philiphaugh."

"Hout," exclaimed another of these discording counsellors, "there's nae great skill needed; just put a lighted peat on the end of a spear, or hayfork, or siclike, and blaw a horn, and cry the gathering-word, and then it's lawful to follow gear into England, and recover it by the strong hand, or to take gear frae some other Englishman, providing ye lift nae mair than's been lifted frae you. That's the auld Border law, made at Dundrennan, in the days of the Black Douglas, Deil ane need doubt it. It's as clear as the sun."

"Come away, then, lads," cried Simon, "get to your geldings, and we'll take auld Cuddie the muckle tasker wi' us; he kens the value o' the stock and plenishing that's been lost. Hobbie's stalls and stakes shall be fou again or night; and if we canna big up the auld house sae soon, we'se lay an English ane as low as Heugh-foot is--and that's fair play, a' the warld ower."

This animating proposal was received with great applause by the younger part of the assemblage, when a whisper ran among them, "There's Hobbie himsell, puir fallow! we'll be guided by him."

The principal sufferer, having now reached the bottom of the hill, pushed on through the crowd, unable, from the tumultuous state of his feelings, to do more than receive and return the grasps of the friendly hands by which his neighbours and kinsmen mutely expressed their sympathy in his misfortune. While he pressed Simon of Hackburn's hand, his anxiety at length found words. "Thank ye, Simon--thank ye, neighbours--I ken what ye wad a' say. But where are they?--Where are--" He stopped, as if afraid even to name the objects of his enquiry; and with a similar feeling, his kinsmen, without reply, pointed to the hut, into which Hobbie precipitated himself with the desperate air of one who is resolved to know the worst at once. A general and powerful expression of sympathy accompanied him. "Ah, puir fallow--puir Hobbie!"

"He'll learn the warst o't now!"

"But I trust Earnscliff will get some speerings o' the puir lassie."

Such were the exclamations of the group, who, having no acknowledged leader to direct their motions, passively awaited the return of the sufferer, and determined to be guided by his directions.

The meeting between Hobbie and his family was in the highest degree affecting. His sisters threw themselves upon him, and almost stifled him with their caresses, as if to prevent his looking round to distinguish the absence of one yet more beloved.

"God help thee, my son! He can help when worldly trust is a broken reed."--Such was the welcome of the matron to her unfortunate grandson. He looked eagerly round, holding two of his sisters by the hand, while the third hung about his neck--"I see you--I count you-- my grandmother, Lilias, Jean, and Annot; but where is--" (he hesitated, and then continued, as if with an effort), "Where is Grace? Surely this is not a time to hide hersell frae me--there's nae time for daffing now."

"O, brother!" and "Our poor Grace!" was the only answer his questions could procure, till his grandmother rose up, and gently disengaged him from the weeping girls, led him to a seat, and with the affecting serenity which sincere piety, like oil sprinkled on the waves, can throw over the most acute feelings, she said, "My bairn, when thy grandfather was killed in the wars, and left me with six orphans around me, with scarce bread to eat, or a roof to cover us, I had strength,--not of mine own--but I had strength given me to say, The Lord's will be done!--My son, our peaceful house was last night broken into by moss-troopers, armed and masked; they have taken and destroyed all, and carried off our dear Grace. Pray for strength to say, His will be done!"

"Mother! mother! urge me not--I cannot--not now I am a sinful man, and of a hardened race. Masked armed--Grace carried off! Gie me my sword, and my father's knapsack--I will have vengeance, if I should go to the pit of darkness to seek it!"

"O my bairn, my bairn! be patient under the rod. Who knows when He may lift His hand off from us? Young Earnscliff, Heaven bless him, has taen the chase, with Davie of Stenhouse, and the first comers. I cried to let house and plenishing burn, and follow the reivers to recover Grace, and Earnscliff and his men were ower the Fell within three hours after the deed. God bless him! he's a real Earnscliff; he's his father's true son--a leal friend."

"A true friend indeed; God bless him!" exclaimed Hobbie; "let's on and away, and take the chase after him."

"O, my child, before you run on danger, let me hear you but say, HIS will be done!"

"Urge me not, mother--not now." He was rushing out, when, looking back, he observed his grandmother make a mute attitude of affliction. He returned hastily, threw himself into her arms, and said, "Yes, mother, I CAN say, HIS will be done, since it will comfort you."

"May He go forth--may He go forth with you, my dear bairn; and O, may He give you cause to say on your return, HIS name be praised!"

"Farewell, mother!--farewell, my dear sisters!" exclaimed Elliot, and rushed out of the house.

CHAPTER VIII.

Now horse and hattock, cried the Laird,-- Now horse and hattock, speedilie; They that winna ride for Telfer's kye, Let them never look in the face o' me. Border Ballad.

"Horse! horse! and spear!" exclaimed Hobbie to his kinsmen. Many a ready foot was in the stirrup; and, while Elliot hastily collected arms and accoutrements, no easy matter in such a confusion, the glen resounded with the approbation of his younger friends.

"Ay, ay!" exclaimed Simon of Hackburn, "that's the gate to take it, Hobbie. Let women sit and greet at hame, men must do as they have been done by; it's the Scripture says't."

"Haud your tongue, sir," said one of the seniors, sternly; "dinna abuse the Word that gate, ye dinna ken what ye speak about."

"Hae ye ony tidings?--Hae ye ony speerings, Hobbie?--O, callants, dinna be ower hasty," said old Dick of the Dingle.

"What signifies preaching to us, e'enow?" said Simon; "if ye canna make help yoursell, dinna keep back them that can."

"Whisht, sir; wad ye take vengeance or ye ken wha has wrang'd ye?"

"D'ye think we dinna ken the road to England as weel as our fathers before us?--All evil comes out o' thereaway--it's an auld saying and a true; and we'll e'en away there, as if the devil was blawing us south."

"We'll follow the track o' Earnscliff's horses ower the waste," cried one Elliot.

"I'll prick them out through the blindest moor in the Border, an there had been a fair held there the day before," said Hugh, the blacksmith of Ringleburn, "for I aye shoe his horse wi' my ain hand."

"Lay on the deer-hounds," cried another "where are they?"

"Hout, man, the sun's been lang up, and the dew is aff the grund -- the scent will never lie."

Hobbie instantly whistled on his hounds, which were roving about the ruins of their old habitation, and filling the air with their doleful howls.

"Now, Killbuck," said Hobbie, "try thy skill this day" and then, as if a light had suddenly broke on him,--"that ill-faur'd goblin spak something o' this! He may ken mair o't, either by villains on earth, or devils below--I'll hae it frae him, if I should cut it out o' his mis-shapen bouk wi' my whinger." He then hastily gave directions to his comrades: "Four o' ye, wi' Simon, haud right forward to Graeme's-gap. If they're English, they'll be for being back that way. The rest disperse by twasome and threesome through the waste, and meet me at the Trysting-pool. Tell my brothers, when they come up, to follow and meet us there. Poor lads, they will hae hearts weelnigh as sair as mine; little think they what a sorrowful house they are bringing their venison to! I'll ride ower Mucklestane-Moor mysell."

"And if I were you," said Dick of the Dingle, "I would speak to Canny Elshie. He can tell you whatever betides in this land, if he's sae minded."

"He SHALL tell me," said Hobbie, who was busy putting his arms in order, "what he kens o' this night's job, or I shall right weel ken wherefore he does not."

"Ay, but speak him fair, my bonny man--speak him fair Hobbie; the like o' him will no bear thrawing. They converse sae muckle wi' thae fractious ghaists and evil spirits, that it clean spoils their temper."

"Let me alane to guide him," answered Hobbie; "there's that in my breast this day, that would ower-maister a' the warlocks on earth, and a' the devils in hell."

And being now fully equipped, he threw himself on his horse, and spurred him at a rapid pace against the steep ascent.

Elliot speedily surmounted the hill, rode down the other side at the same rate, crossed a wood, and traversed a long glen, ere he at length regained Mucklestane-Moor. As he was obliged, in the course of his journey, to relax his speed in consideration of the labour which his horse might still have to undergo, he had time to consider maturely in what manner he should address the Dwarf, in order to extract from him the knowledge which he supposed him to be in possession of concerning the authors of his misfortunes. Hobbie, though blunt, plain of speech, and hot of disposition, like most of his countrymen, was by no means deficient in the shrewdness which is also their characteristic. He reflected, that from what he had observed on the memorable night when the Dwarf was first seen, and from the conduct of that mysterious being ever since, he was likely to be rendered even more obstinate in his sullenness by threats and violence.

"I'll speak him fair," he said, "as auld Dickon advised me. Though folk say he has a league wi' Satan, he canna be sic an incarnate devil as no to take some pity in a case like mine; and folk threep he'll whiles do good, charitable sort o' things. I'll keep my heart doun as weel as I can, and stroke him wi' the hair; and if the warst come to the warst, it's but wringing the head o' him about at last."

In this disposition of accommodation he approached the hut of the Solitary.

The old man was not upon his seat of audience, nor could Hobbie perceive him in his garden, or enclosures.

"He's gotten into his very keep," said Hobbie, "maybe to be out o' the gate; but I'se pu' it doun about his lugs, if I canna win at him otherwise."

Having thus communed with himself, he raised his voice, and invoked Elshie in a tone as supplicating as his conflicting feelings would permit. "Elshie, my gude friend!" No reply. "Elshie, canny Father Elshie!" The Dwarf remained mute. "Sorrow be in the crooked carcass of thee!" said the Borderer between his teeth; and then again attempting a soothing tone,--"Good Father Elshie, a most miserable creature desires some counsel of your wisdom."

"The better!" answered the shrill and discordant voice of the Dwarf through a very small window, resembling an arrow slit, which he had constructed near the door of his dwelling, and through which he could see any one who approached it, without the possibility of their looking in upon him.

"The better!" said Hobbie impatiently; "what is the better, Elshie? Do you not hear me tell you I am the most miserable wretch living?"

"And do you not hear me tell you it is so much the better! and did I not tell you this morning, when you thought yourself so happy, what an evening was coming upon you?"

"That ye did e'en," replied Hobbie, "and that gars me come to you for advice now; they that foresaw the trouble maun ken the cure."

"I know no cure for earthly trouble," returned the Dwarf "or, if I did, why should I help others, when none hath aided me? Have I not lost wealth, that would have bought all thy barren hills a hundred times over? rank, to which thine is as that of a peasant? society, where there was an interchange of all that was amiable--of all that was intellectual? Have I not lost all this? Am I not residing here, the veriest outcast on the face of Nature, in the most hideous and most solitary of her retreats, myself more hideous than all that is around me? And why should other worms complain to me when they are trodden on, since I am myself lying crushed and writhing under the chariot-wheel?"

"Ye may have lost all this," answered Hobbie, in the bitterness of emotion; "land and friends, goods and gear; ye may hae lost them a',--but ye ne'er can hae sae sair a heart as mine, for ye ne'er lost nae Grace Armstrong. And now my last hopes are gane, and I shall ne'er see her mair."

This he said in the tone of deepest emotion--and there followed a long pause, for the mention of his bride's name had overcome the more angry and irritable feelings of poor Hobbie. Ere he had again addressed the Solitary, the bony hand and long fingers of the latter, holding a large leathern bag, was thrust forth at the small window, and as it unclutched the burden, and let it drop with a clang upon the ground, his harsh voice again addressed Elliot.

"There--there lies a salve for every human ill; so, at least, each human wretch readily thinks.--Begone; return twice as wealthy as thou wert before yesterday, and torment me no more with questions, complaints, or thanks; they are alike odious to me."

"It is a' gowd, by Heaven!" said Elliot, having glanced at the contents; and then again addressing the Hermit, "Muckle obliged for your goodwill; and I wad blithely gie you a bond for some o' the siller, or a wadset ower the lands o' Wideopen. But I dinna ken, Elshie; to be free wi' you, I dinna like to use siller unless I kend it

71

was decently come by; and maybe it might turn into sclate-stanes, and cheat some poor man."

"Ignorant idiot!" retorted the Dwarf; "the trash is as genuine poison as ever was dug out of the bowels of the earth. Take it --use it, and may it thrive with you as it hath done with me!"

"But I tell you," said Elliot, "it wasna about the gear that I was consulting you,--it was a braw barn-yard, doubtless, and thirty head of finer cattle there werena on this side of the Catrail; but let the gear gang,--if ye could but gie me speerings o' puir Grace, I would be content to be your slave for life, in onything that didna touch my salvation. O, Elshie, speak, man, speak!"

"Well, then," answered the Dwarf, as if worn out by his importunity, "since thou hast not enough of woes of thine own, but must needs seek to burden thyself with those of a partner, seek her whom thou hast lost in the WEST."

"In the WEST? That's a wide word."

"It is the last," said the Dwarf, which I design to utter;" and he drew the shutters of his window, leaving Hobbie to make the most of the hint he had given.

The west! the west!--thought Elliot; the country is pretty quiet down that way, unless it were Jock o' the Todholes; and he's ower auld now for the like o' thae jobs.--West!--By My life, it must be Westburnflat. "Elshie, just tell me one word. Am I right? Is it Westburnflat? If I am wrang, say sae. I wadna like to wyte an innocent neighbour wi' violence--No answer?--It must be the Red Reiver--I didna think he wad hae ventured on me, neither, and sae mony kin as there's o' us--I am thinking he'll hae some better backing than his Cumberland friends.--Fareweel to you, Elshie, and mony thanks--I downa be fashed wi' the siller e'en now, for I maun awa' to meet my friends at the Trysting-place-- Sae, if ye carena to open the window, ye can fetch it in after I'm awa'."

Still there was no reply.

"He's deaf, or he's daft, or he's baith; but I hae nae time to stay to claver wi' him."

72

And off rode Hobbie Elliot towards the place of rendezvous which he had named to his friends.

Four or five riders were already gathered at the Trysting pool. They stood in close consultation together, while their horses were permitted to graze among the poplars which overhung the broad still pool. A more numerous party were seen coming from the southward. It proved to be Earnscliff and his party, who had followed the track of the cattle as far as the English border, but had halted on the information that a considerable force was drawn together under some of the Jacobite gentlemen in that district, and there were tidings of insurrection in different parts of Scotland. This took away from the act which had been perpetrated the appearance of private animosity, or love of plunder; and Earnscliff was now disposed to regard it as a symptom of civil war. The young gentleman greeted Hobbie with the most sincere sympathy, and informed him of the news he had received.

"Then, may I never stir frae the bit," said Elliot, "if auld Ellieslaw is not at the bottom o' the haill villainy! Ye see he's leagued wi' the Cumberland Catholics; and that agrees weel wi' what Elshie hinted about Westburnflat, for Ellieslaw aye protected him, and he will want to harry and disarm the country about his ain hand before he breaks out."

Some now remembered that the party of ruffians had been heard to say they were acting for James VIII., and were charged to disarm all rebels. Others had heard Westburnflat boast, in drinking parties, that Ellieslaw would soon be in arms for the Jacobite cause, and that he himself was to hold a command under him, and that they would be bad neighbours for young Earnscliff; and all that stood out for the established government. The result was a strong belief that Westburnflat had headed the party under Ellieslaw's orders; and they resolved to proceed instantly to the house of the former, and, if possible, to secure his person. They were by this time joined by so many of their dispersed friends, that their number amounted to upwards of twenty horsemen, well mounted, and tolerably, though variously, armed.

A brook, which issued from a narrow glen among the hills, entered, at Westburnflat, upon the open marshy level, which, expanding about half a mile in every direction, gives name to the spot. In this place the character of the stream becomes changed, and, from being a lively brisk-running mountain-torrent, it stagnates, like a blue swollen snake, in dull deep windings, through the swampy level. On the side of the stream, and nearly about the centre of the plain, arose the tower of Westburnflat, one of the few remaining strongholds formerly so numerous upon the Borders. The ground upon which it stood was gently elevated above the marsh for the space of about a hundred yards, affording an esplanade of dry turf, which extended itself in the immediate neighbourhood of the tower; but, beyond which, the surface presented to strangers was that of an impassable and dangerous bog. The owner of the tower and his inmates alone knew the winding and intricate paths, which, leading over ground that was comparatively sound, admitted visitors to his residence. But among the party which were assembled under Earnscliff's directions, there was more than one person qualified to act as a guide. For although the owner's character and habits of life were generally known, yet the laxity of feeling with respect to property prevented his being looked on with the abhorrence with which he must have been regarded in a more civilized country. He was considered, among his more peaceable neighbours, pretty much as a gambler, cock-fighter, or horse-jockey would be regarded at the present day; a person, of course, whose habits were to be condemned, and his society, in general, avoided, yet who could not be considered as marked with the indelible infamy attached to his profession, where laws have been habitually observed. And their indignation was awakened against him upon this occasion, not so much on account of the general nature of the transaction, which was just such as was to be expected from this marauder, as that the violence had been perpetrated upon a neighbour against whom he had no cause of quarrel,--against a friend of their own, --above all, against one of the name of Elliot, to which clan most of them belonged. It was not, therefore, wonderful, that there should be several in the band pretty well acquainted with the locality of his habitation, and capable of giving such directions and guidance as soon placed the whole party on the open space of firm ground in front of the Tower of Westburnflat.

CHAPTER IX.

So spak the knicht; the geaunt sed, Lend forth with the, the sely maid, And mak me quile of the and sche; For glaunsing ee, or brow so brent, Or cheek with rose and lilye blent, Me lists not ficht with the. ROMANCE OF THE FALCON.

The tower, before which the party now stood, was a small square building, of the most gloomy aspect. The walls were of great thickness, and the windows, or slits which served the purpose of windows, seemed rather calculated to afford the defenders the means of employing missile weapons, than for admitting air or light to the apartments within. A small battlement projected over the walls on every side, and afforded farther advantage of defence by its niched parapet, within which arose a steep roof, flagged with grey stones. A single turret at one angle, defended by a door studded with huge iron nails, rose above the battlement, and gave access to the roof from within, by the spiral staircase which it enclosed. It seemed to the party that their motions were watched by some one concealed within this turret; and they were confirmed in their belief when, through a narrow loophole, a female hand was seen to wave a handkerchief, as if by way of signal to them. Hobbie was almost out of his senses with joy and eagerness.

"It was Grace's hand and arm," he said; "I can swear to it amang a thousand. There is not the like of it on this side of the Lowdens-- We'll have her out, lads, if we should carry off the Tower of Westburnflat stane by stane."

Earnscliff, though he doubted the possibility of recognising a fair maiden's hand at such a distance from the eye of the lover, would say nothing to damp his friend's animated hopes, and it was resolved to summon the garrison.

The shouts of the party, and the winding of one or two horns, at length brought to a loophole, which flanked the entrance, the haggard face of an old woman.

"That's the Reiver's mother," said one of the Elliots; "she's ten times waur than himsell, and is wyted for muckle of the ill he does about the country."

"Wha are ye? what d'ye want here?" were the queries of the respectable progenitor.

"We are seeking William Graeme of Westburnflat," said Earnscliff.

"He's no at hame," returned the old dame.

"When did he leave home?" pursued Earnscliff.

"I canna tell," said the portress.

"When will he return?" said Hobbie Elliot.

"I dinna ken naething about it," replied the inexorable guardian of the keep.

"Is there anybody within the tower with you?" again demanded Earnscliff.

"Naebody but mysell and baudrons," said the old woman.

"Then open the gate and admit us," said Earnscliff; "I am a justice of peace, and in search of the evidence of a felony."

"Deil be in their fingers that draws a bolt for ye," retorted the portress; "for mine shall never do it. Thinkna ye shame o' yoursells, to come here siccan a band o' ye, wi' your swords, and spears, and steel-caps, to frighten a lone widow woman?"

"Our information," said Earnscliff; "is positive; we are seeking goods which have been forcibly carried off, to a great amount."

"And a young woman, that's been cruelly made prisoner, that's worth mair than a' the gear, twice told," said Hobbie.

"And I warn you." continued Earnscliff, "that your only way to prove your son's innocence is to give us quiet admittance to search the house."

"And what will ye do, if I carena to thraw the keys, or draw the bolts, or open the grate to sic a clamjamfrie?" said the old dame, scoffingly.

"Force our way with the king's keys, and break the neck of every living soul we find in the house, if ye dinna gie it ower forthwith!" menaced the incensed Hobbie.

"Threatened folks live lang," said the hag, in the same tone of irony; "there's the iron grate--try your skeel on't, lads--it has kept out as gude men as you or now."

So saying, she laughed, and withdrew from the aperture through which she had held the parley.

The besiegers now opened a serious consultation. The immense thickness of the walls, and the small size of the windows, might, for a time, have even resisted cannon-shot. The entrance was secured, first, by a strong grated door, composed entirely of hammered iron, of such ponderous strength as seemed calculated to resist any force that could be brought against it. "Pinches or forehammers will never pick upon't," said Hugh, the blacksmith of Ringleburn; "ye might as weel batter at it wi' pipe-staples."

Within the doorway, and at the distance of nine feet, which was the solid thickness of the wall, there was a second door of oak, crossed, both breadth and lengthways, with clenched bars of iron, and studded full of broad-headed nails. Besides all these defences, they were by no means confident in the truth of the old dame's assertion, that she alone composed the garrison. The more knowing of the party had observed hoof-marks in the track by which they approached the tower, which seemed to indicate that several persons had very lately passed in that direction.

To all these difficulties was added their want of means for attacking the place. There was no hope of procuring ladders long enough to reach the battlements, and the windows, besides being very narrow, were secured with iron bars. Scaling was therefore out of the question; mining was still more so, for want of tools and gunpowder; neither were the besiegers provided with food, means of shelter, or other conveniences, which might have enabled them to convert the siege into a blockade; and there would, at any rate, have been a risk of relief from some of the marauder's comrades. Hobbie grinded and gnashed his teeth, as, walking round the fastness, he could devise no means of making a forcible entry. At length he suddenly exclaimed, "And what for no do as our fathers did lang syne?--Put hand to the wark, lads. Let us cut up bushes and briers, pile them before the door and set fire to them, and smoke that auld devil's dam as if she were to be reested for bacon."

All immediately closed with this proposal, and some went to work with swords and knives to cut down the alder and hawthorn bushes which grew by the side of the sluggish stream, many of which were sufficiently decayed and dried for their purpose, while others began to collect them in a large stack, properly disposed for burning, as close to the iron-grate as they could be piled. Fire was speedily obtained from one of their guns, and Hobbie was already advancing to the pile with a kindled brand, when the surly face of the robber, and the muzzle of a musquetoon, were partially shown at a shot-hole which flanked the entrance. "Mony thanks to ye," he said, scoffingly, "for collecting sae muckle winter eilding for us; but if ye step a foot nearer it wi' that lunt, it's be the dearest step ye ever made in your days."

"We'll sune see that," said Hobbie, advancing fearlessly with the torch.

The marauder snapped his piece at him, which, fortunately for our honest friend, did not go off; while Earnscliff, firing at the same moment at the narrow aperture and slight mark afforded by the robber's face, grazed the side of his head with a bullet. He had apparently calculated upon his post affording him more security, for he no sooner felt the wound, though a very slight one, than he requested a parley, and demanded to know what they meant by attacking in this fashion a peaceable and honest man, and shedding his blood in that lawless manner?

"We want your prisoner," said Earnscliff, "to be delivered up to us in safety,"

"And what concern have you with her?" replied the marauder.

"That," retorted Earnscliff, "you, who are detaining her by force, have no right to enquire."

"Aweel, I think I can gie a guess," said the robber. "Weel, sirs, I am laith to enter into deadly feud with you by spilling ony of your bluid, though Earnscliff hasna stopped to shed mine --and he can hit a mark to a groat's breadth--so, to prevent mair skaith, I am willing to deliver up the prisoner, since nae less will please you."

"And Hobbie's gear?" cried Simon of Hackburn. "D'ye think you're to be free to plunder the faulds and byres of a gentle Elliot, as if they were an auld wife's hens'-cavey?"

"As I live by bread," replied Willie of Westburnflat "As I live by bread, I have not a single cloot o' them! They're a' ower the march lang syne; there's no a horn o' them about the tower. But I'll see what o' them can be gotten back, and I'll take this day twa days to meet Hobbie at the Castleton wi' twa friends on ilka side, and see to make an agreement about a' the wrang he can wyte me wi'."

"Ay, ay," said Elliot, "that will do weel eneugh."--And then aside to his kinsman, "Murrain on the gear! Lordsake, man! say nought about them. Let us but get puir Grace out o' that auld hellicat's clutches."

"Will ye gie me your word, Earnscliff," said the marauder, who still lingered at the shot-hole, "your faith and troth, with hand and glove, that I am free to come and free to gae, with five minutes to open the grate, and five minutes to steek it and to draw the bolts? less winna do, for they want creishing sairly. Will ye do this?"

"You shall have full time," said Earnscliff; "I plight my faith and troth, my hand and my glove."

"Wait there a moment, then," said Westburnflat; "or hear ye, I wad rather ye wad fa' back a pistol-shot from the door. It's no that I mistrust your word, Earnscliff; but it's best to be sure."

O, friend, thought Hobbie to himself, as he drew back, an I had you but on Turner's-holm, [There is a level meadow, on the very margin of the two kingdoms, called Turner's-holm, just where the brook called Crissop joins the Liddel. It is said to have derived its name as being a place frequently assigned for tourneys, during the ancient Border times.] and naebody by but twa honest lads to see fair play, I wad make ye wish ye had broken your leg ere ye had touched beast or body that belanged to me!

"He has a white feather in his wing this same Westburnflat, after a'," said Simon of Hackburn, somewhat scandalized by his ready surrender.--"He'll ne'er fill his father's boots."

In the meanwhile, the inner door of the tower was opened, and the mother of the freebooter appeared in the space betwixt that and the outer grate. Willie himself was next seen, leading forth a female, and the old woman, carefully bolting the grate behind them, remained on the post as a sort of sentinel.

"Ony ane or twa o' ye come forward," said the outlaw, "and take her frae my hand haill and sound."

Hobbie advanced eagerly, to meet his betrothed bride. Earnscliff followed more slowly, to guard against treachery. Suddenly Hobbie slackened his pace in the deepest mortification, while that of Earnscliff was hastened by impatient surprise. It was not Grace Armstrong, but Miss Isabella Vere, whose liberation had been effected by their appearance before the tower.

"Where is Grace? where is Grace Armstrong?" exclaimed Hobbie, in the extremity of wrath and indignation.

"Not in my hands," answered Westburnflat; "ye may search the tower, if ye misdoubt me."

"You false villain, you shall account for her, or die on the spot," said Elliot, presenting his gun.

But his companions, who now came up, instantly disarmed him of his weapon, exclaiming, all at once, "Hand and glove! faith and troth! Haud a care, Hobbie we maun keep our faith wi' Westburnflat, were he the greatest rogue ever rode."

Thus protected, the outlaw recovered his audacity, which had been somewhat daunted by the menacing gesture of Elliot.

"I have kept my word, sirs," he said, "and I look to have nae wrang amang ye. If this is no the prisoner ye sought," he said, addressing Earnscliff, "ye'll render her back to me again. I am answerable for her to those that aught her."

"For God's sake, Mr. Earnscliff, protect me!" said Miss Vere, clinging to her deliverer; "do not you abandon one whom the whole world seems to have abandoned."

"Fear nothing," whispered Earnscliff, "I will protect you with my life." Then turning to Westburnflat, "Villain!" he said, "how dared you to insult this lady?"

"For that matter, Earnscliff," answered the freebooter, "I can answer to them that has better right to ask me than you have; but if you come with an armed force, and take her awa' from them that her friends lodged her wi', how will you answer THAT--But it's your ain affair--Nae single man can keep a tower against twenty --A' the men o' the Mearns downa do mair than they dow."

"He lies most falsely," said Isabella; "he carried me off by violence from my father."

"Maybe he only wanted ye to think sae, hinny," replied the robber; "but it's nae business o' mine, let it be as it may.--So ye winna resign her back to me?"

"Back to you, fellow? Surely no," answered Earnscliff; "I will protect Miss Vere, and escort her safely wherever she is pleased to be conveyed."

"Ay, ay, maybe you and her hae settled that already," said Willie of Westburnflat.

"And Grace?" interrupted Hobbie, shaking himself loose from the friends who had been preaching to him the sanctity of the safe-conduct, upon the faith of which the freebooter had ventured from his tower,--"Where's Grace" and he rushed on the marauder, sword in hand.

Westburnflat, thus pressed, after calling out, "Godsake, Hobbie, hear me a gliff!" fairly turned his back and fled. His mother stood ready to open and shut the grate; but Hobbie struck at the freebooter as he entered with so much force, that the sword made a considerable cleft in the lintel of the vaulted door, which is still shown as a memorial of the superior strength of those who lived in the days of yore. Ere Hobbie could repeat the blow, the door was shut and secured, and he was compelled to retreat to his companions, who were now preparing to break up the siege of Westburnflat. They insisted upon his accompanying them in their return.

"Ye hae broken truce already," said old Dick of the Dingle; "an we takena the better care, ye'll play mair gowk's tricks, and make yoursell the laughing-stock of the haill country, besides having your friends charged with slaughter under trust. Bide till the meeting at Castleton, as ye hae greed; and if he disna make ye amends, then we'll hae it out o' his heart's blood. But let us gang reasonably to wark and keep our tryst, and I'se warrant we get back Grace, and the kye an' a'."

This cold-blooded reasoning went ill down with the unfortunate lover; but, as he could only obtain the assistance of his neighbours and kinsmen on their own terms, he was compelled to acquiesce in their notions of good faith and regular procedure.

Earnscliff now requested the assistance of a few of the party to convey Miss Vere to her father's castle of Ellieslaw, to which she was peremptory in desiring to be conducted. This was readily granted; and five or six young men agreed to attend him as an escort. Hobbie was not of the number. Almost heart-broken by the events of the day, and his final disappointment, he returned moodily home to take such measures as he could for the sustenance and protection of his family, and to arrange with his neighbours the farther steps which should be adopted for the recovery of Grace Armstrong. The rest of the party dispersed in different directions, as soon as they had crossed the morass. The outlaw and his mother watched them from the tower, until they entirely disappeared.

CHAPTER X.

I left my ladye's bower last night-- It was clad in wreaths of snaw,--
I'll seek it when the sun is bright, And sweet the roses blaw. OLD
BALLAD.

Incensed at what he deemed the coldness of his friends, in a cause
which interested him so nearly, Hobbie had shaken himself free of
their company, and was now on his solitary road homeward. "The
fiend founder thee!" said he, as he spurred impatiently his over-
fatigued and stumbling horse; "thou art like a' the rest o' them. Hae I
not bred thee, and fed thee, and dressed thee wi' mine ain hand, and
wouldst thou snapper now and break my neck at my utmost need?
But thou'rt e'en like the lave--the farthest off o' them a' is my cousin
ten times removed, and day or night I wad hae served them wi' my
best blood; and now, I think they show mair regard to the common
thief of Westburnflat than to their ain kinsman. But I should see the
lights now in Heugh-foot--Wae's me!" he continued, recollecting
himself, "there will neither coal nor candle-light shine in the Heugh-
foot ony mair! An it werena for my mother and sisters, and poor
Grace, I could find in my heart to put spurs to the beast, and loup
ower the scaur into the water to make an end o't a'."--In this
disconsolate mood he turned his horse's bridle towards the cottage
in which his family had found refuge.

As he approached the door, he heard whispering and tittering
amongst his sisters. "The deevil's in the women," said poor Hobbie;
"they would nicker, and laugh, and giggle, if their best friend was
lying a corp--and yet I am glad they can keep up their hearts sae
weel, poor silly things; but the dirdum fa's on me, to be sure, and no
on them."

While he thus meditated, he was engaged in fastening up his horse
in a shed. "Thou maun do without horse-sheet and surcingle now,
lad," he said, addressing the animal; "you and me hae had a
downcome alike; we had better hae fa'en i, the deepest pool o'
Tarras."

He was interrupted by the youngest of his sisters, who came running
out, and, speaking in a constrained voice, as if to stifle some emotion,
called out to him, "What are ye doing there, Hobbie, fiddling about
the naig, and there's ane frae Cumberland been waiting here for ye
this hour and mair? Haste ye in, man; I'll take off the saddle."

"Ane frae Cumberland!" exclaimed Elliot; and putting the bridle of his horse into the hand of his sister, he rushed into the cottage. "Where is he? where is he!" he exclaimed, glancing eagerly around, and seeing only females; "Did he bring news of Grace?"

"He doughtna bide an instant langer," said the elder sister, still with a suppressed laugh.

"Hout fie, bairns!" said the old lady, with something of a good-humoured reproof, "ye shouldna vex your billy Hobbie that way.-- Look round, my bairn, and see if there isna ane here mair than ye left this morning."

Hobbie looked eagerly round. "There's you, and the three titties."

"There's four of us now, Hobbie, lad," said the youngest, who at this moment entered.

In an instant Hobbie had in his arms Grace Armstrong, who, with one of his sister's plaids around her, had passed unnoticed at his first entrance. "How dared you do this?" said Hobbie.

"It wasna my fault," said Grace, endeavouring to cover her face with her hands to hide at once her blushes, and escape the storm of hearty kisses with which her bridegroom punished her simple stratagem,-- "It wasna my fault, Hobbie; ye should kiss Jeanie and the rest o' them, for they hae the wyte o't."

"And so I will," said Hobbie, and embraced and kissed his sisters and grandmother a hundred times, while the whole party half-laughed, half-cried, in the extremity of their joy. "I am the happiest man," said Hobbie, throwing himself down on a seat, almost exhausted,--"I am the happiest man in the world!"

"Then, O my dear bairn," said the good old dame, who lost no opportunity of teaching her lesson of religion at those moments when the heart was best open to receive it,--"Then, O my son, give praise to Him that brings smiles out o' tears and joy out o' grief, as He brought light out o' darkness and the world out o' naething. Was it not my word, that if ye could say His will be done, ye might hae cause to say His name be praised?"

"It was--it was your word, grannie; and I do praise Him for His mercy, and for leaving me a good parent when my ain were gane," said honest Hobbie, taking her hand, "that puts me in mind to think of Him, baith in happiness and distress."

There was a solemn pause of one or two minutes employed in the exercise of mental devotion, which expressed, in purity and sincerity, the gratitude of the affectionate family to that Providence who had unexpectedly restored to their embraces the friend whom they had lost.

Hobbie's first enquiries were concerning the adventures which Grace had undergone. They were told at length, but amounted in substance to this:--That she was awaked by the noise which the ruffians made in breaking into the house, and by the resistance made by one or two of the servants, which was soon overpowered; that, dressing herself hastily, she ran downstairs, and having seen, in the scuffle, Westburnflat's vizard drop off, imprudently named him by his name, and besought him for mercy; that the ruffian instantly stopped her mouth, dragged her from the house, and placed her on horseback, behind one of his associates.

"I'll break the accursed neck of him," said Hobbie, "if there werena another Graeme in the land but himsell!"

She proceeded to say, that she was carried southward along with the party, and the spoil which they drove before them, until they had crossed the Border. Suddenly a person, known to her as a kinsman of Westburnflat, came riding very fast after the marauders, and told their leader, that his cousin had learnt from a sure hand that no luck would come of it, unless the lass was restored to her friends. After some discussion, the chief of the party seemed to acquiesce. Grace was placed behind her new guardian, who pursued in silence, and with great speed, the least-frequented path to the Heugh-foot, and ere evening closed, set down the fatigued and terrified damsel within a quarter of a mile of the dwelling of her friends. Many and sincere were the congratulations which passed on all sides.

As these emotions subsided, less pleasing considerations began to intrude themselves.

"This is a miserable place for ye a'," said Hobbie, looking around him; "I can sleep weel eneugh mysell outby beside the naig, as I hae done mony a lang night on the hills; but how ye are to put yoursells up, I canna see! And what's waur, I canna mend it; and what's waur than a', the morn may come, and the day after that, without your being a bit better off."

"It was a cowardly cruel thing," said one of the sisters, looking round, "to harry a puir family to the bare wa's this gate."

"And leave us neither stirk nor stot," said the youngest brother, who now entered, "nor sheep nor lamb, nor aught that eats grass and corn."

"If they had ony quarrel wi' us," said Harry, the second brother, "were we na ready to have fought it out? And that we should have been a' frae hame, too,--ane and a' upon the hill--Odd, an we had been at hame, Will Graeme's stamach shouldna hae wanted its morning; but it's biding him, is it na, Hobbie?"

"Our neighbours hae taen a day at the Castleton to gree wi' him at the sight o' men," said Hobbie, mournfully; "they behoved to have it a' their ain gate, or there was nae help to be got at their hands."

"To gree wi' him!" exclaimed both his brothers at once, "after siccan an act of stouthrife as hasna been heard o' in the country since the auld riding days!"

"Very true, billies, and my blood was e'en boiling at it; but the sight o' Grace Armstrong has settled it brawly."

"But the stocking, Hobbie'" said John Elliot; "we're utterly ruined. Harry and I hae been to gather what was on the outby land, and there's scarce a cloot left. I kenna how we're to carry on--We maun a' gang to the wars, I think. Westburnflat hasna the means, e'en if he had the will, to make up our loss; there's nae mends to be got out o' him, but what ye take out o' his banes. He hasna a four-footed creature but the vicious blood thing he rides on, and that's sair trash'd wi' his night wark. We are ruined stoop and roop."

Hobbie cast a mournful glance on Grace Armstrong, who returned it with a downcast look and a gentle sigh.

"Dinna be cast down, bairns," said the grandmother, "we hae gude friends that winna forsake us in adversity. There's Sir Thomas Kittleloof is my third cousin by the mother's side, and he has come by a hantle siller, and been made a knight-baronet into the bargain, for being ane o' the commissioners at the Union."

"He wadna gie a bodle to save us frae famishing," said Hobbie; "and, if he did, the bread that I bought wi't would stick in my throat, when I thought it was part of the price of puir auld Scotland's crown and independence."

"There's the Laird o' Dunder, ane o' the auldest families in Tiviotdale."

"He's in the tolbooth, mother--he's in the Heart of Mid-Louden for a thousand merk he borrowed from Saunders Wyliecoat the writer."

"Poor man!" exclaimed Mrs. Elliot, "can we no send him something, Hobbie?"

"Ye forget, grannie, ye forget we want help oursells," said Hobbie, somewhat peevishly.

"Troth did I, hinny," replied the good-natured lady, "just at the instant; it's sae natural to think on ane's blude relations before themsells;--But there's young Earnscliff."

"He has ower little o' his ain; and siccan a name to keep up, it wad be a shame," said Hobbie, "to burden him wi' our distress. And I'll tell ye, grannie, it's needless to sit rhyming ower the style of a' your kith, kin, and allies, as if there was a charm in their braw names to do us good; the grandees hae forgotten us, and those of our ain degree hae just little eneugh to gang on wi' themsells; ne'er a friend hae we that can, or will, help us to stock the farm again."

"Then, Hobbie, me maun trust in Him that can raise up friends and fortune out o' the bare moor, as they say."

Hobbie sprung upon his feet. "Ye are right, grannie!" he exclaimed; "ye are right. I do ken a friend on the bare moor, that baith can and will help us--The turns o' this day hae dung my head clean hirdie-girdie. I left as muckle gowd lying on Mucklestane-Moor this morning as would plenish the house and stock the Heugh-foot twice ower, and I am certain sure Elshie wadna grudge us the use of it."

"Elshie!" said his grandmother in astonishment; "what Elshie do you mean?"

"What Elshie should I mean, but Canny Elshie, the Wight o' Mucklestane," replied Hobbie.

"God forfend, my bairn, you should gang to fetch water out o' broken cisterns, or seek for relief frae them that deal wi' the Evil One! There was never luck in their gifts, nor grace in their paths. And the haill country kens that body Elshie's an unco man. O, if there was the law, and the douce quiet administration of justice, that makes a kingdom flourish in righteousness, the like o' them suldna be suffered to live! The wizard and the witch are the abomination and the evil thing in the land."

"Troth, mother," answered Hobbie, "ye may say what ye like, but I am in the mind that witches and warlocks havena half the power they had lang syne; at least, sure am I, that ae ill-deviser, like auld Ellieslaw, or ae ill-doer, like that d--d villain Westburnflat, is a greater plague and abomination in a country- side than a haill curnie o' the warst witches that ever capered on a broomstick, or played cantrips on Fastern's E'en. It wad hae been lang or Elshie had burnt down my house and barns, and I am determined to try if he will do aught to build them up again. He's weel kend a skilfu' man ower a' the country, as far as Brough under Stanmore."

"Bide a wee, my bairn; mind his benefits havena thriven wi' a'body. Jock Howden died o' the very same disorder Elshie pretended to cure him of, about the fa' o' the leaf; and though he helped Lambside's cow weel out o' the moor-ill, yet the louping-ill's been sairer amane; his sheep than ony season before. And then I have heard he uses sic words abusing human nature, that's like a fleeing in the face of Providence; and ye mind ye said yoursell, the first time ye ever saw him, that he was mair like a bogle than a living thing."

"Hout, mother," said Hobbie, "Elshie's no that bad a chield; he's a grewsome spectacle for a crooked disciple, to be sure, and a rough talker, but his bark is waur than his bite; sae, if I had anes something to eat, for I havena had a morsel ower my throat this day, I wad streek mysell down for twa or three hours aside the beast, and be on and awa' to Mucklestane wi' the first skreigh o' morning."

"And what for no the night, Hobbie," said Harry, "and I will ride wi' ye?"

"My naig is tired," said Hobbie.

"Ye may take mine, then," said John.

"But I am a wee thing wearied mysell."

"You wearied?" said Harry; "shame on ye! I have kend ye keep the saddle four-and-twenty hours thegither, and ne'er sic a word as weariness in your wame."

"The night's very dark," said Hobbie, rising and looking through the casement of the cottage; "and, to speak truth, and shame the deil, though Elshie's a real honest fallow, yet somegate I would rather take daylight wi' me when I gang to visit him."

This frank avowal put a stop to further argument; and Hobbie, having thus compromised matters between the rashness of his brother's counsel, and the timid cautions which he received from his grandmother, refreshed himself with such food as the cottage afforded; and, after a cordial salutation all round, retired to the shed, and stretched himself beside his trusty palfrey. His brothers shared between them some trusses of clean straw, disposed in the stall usually occupied by old Annaple's cow; and the females arranged themselves for repose as well as the accommodations of the cottage would permit.

With the first dawn of morning, Hobbie arose; and, having rubbed down and saddled his horse, he set forth to Mucklestane-Moor. He avoided the company of either of his brothers, from an idea that the Dwarf was most propitious to those who visited him alone.

"The creature," said he to himself, as he went along, "is no neighbourly; ae body at a time is fully mair than he weel can abide. I wonder if he's looked out o' the crib o' him to gather up the bag o' siller. If he hasna done that, it will hae been a braw windfa' for somebody, and I'll be finely flung.--Come, Tarras," said he to his horse, striking him at the same time with his spur, "make mair fit, man; we maun be first on the field if we can."

He was now on the heath, which began to be illuminated by the beams of the rising sun; the gentle declivity which he was descending presented him a distinct, though distant view, of the Dwarf's dwelling. The door opened, and Hobbie witnessed with his own eyes that phenomenon which he had frequently heard mentioned. Two human figures (if that of the Dwarf could be termed such) issued from the solitary abode of the Recluse, and stood as if in converse together in the open air. The taller form then stooped, as if taking something up which lay beside the door of the hut, then both moved forward a little way, and again halted, as in deep conference. All Hobbie's superstitious terrors revived on witnessing this'spectacle. That the Dwarf would open his dwelling to a mortal guest, was as improbable as that any one would choose voluntarily to be his nocturnal visitor; and, under full conviction that he beheld a wizard holding intercourse with his familiar spirit, Hobbie pulled in at once his breath and his bridle, resolved not to incur the indignation of either by a hasty intrusion on their conference. They were probably aware of his approach, for he had not halted for a moment before the Dwarf returned to his cottage; and the taller figure who had accompanied him, glided round the enclosure of the garden, and seemed to disappear from the eyes of the admiring Hobbie.

"Saw ever mortal the like o' that!" said Elliot; "but my case is desperate, sae, if he were Beelzebub himsell, I'se venture down the brae on him."

Yet, notwithstanding his assumed courage, he slackened his pace, when, nearly upon the very spot where he had last seen the tall figure, he discerned, as if lurking among the long heather, a small black rough-looking object, like a terrier dog.

"He has nae dog that ever I heard of," said Hobbie, "but mony a deil about his hand--lord forgie me for saying sic a word!--It keeps its grund, be what it like--I'm judging it's a badger; but whae kens what shapes thae bogies will take to fright a body? it will maybe start up like a lion or a crocodile when I come nearer. I'se e'en drive a stage at it, for if it change its shape when I'm ower near, Tarras will never stand it; and it will be ower muckle to hae him and the deil to fight wi' baith at ance."

He therefore cautiously threw a stone at the object, which continued motionless. "It's nae living thing, after a'," said Hobbie, approaching, "but the very bag o' siller he flung out o' the window yesterday! and that other queer lang creature has just brought it sae muckle farther on the way to me. He then advanced and lifted the heavy fur pouch, which was quite full of gold. "Mercy on us!" said Hobbie, whose heart fluttered between glee at the revival of his hopes and prospects in life, and suspicion of the purpose for which this assistance was afforded him---"Mercy on us! it's an awfu' thing to touch what has been sae lately in the claws of something no canny, I canna shake mysell loose o' the belief that there has been some jookery- paukery of Satan's in a' this; but I am determined to conduct mysell like an honest man and a good Christian, come o't what will."

He advanced accordingly to the cottage door, and having knocked repeatedly without receiving any answer, he at length elevated his voice and addressed the inmate of the hut. "Elshie! Father Elshie! I ken ye're within doors, and wauking, for I saw ye at the door-cheek as I cam ower the bent; will ye come out and speak just a gliff to ane that has mony thanks to gie ye?--It was a' true ye tell'd me about Westburnflat; but he's sent back Grace safe and skaithless, sae there's nae ill happened yet but what may be suffered or sustained;--Wad ye but come out a gliff; man, or but say ye're listening?--Aweel, since ye winna answer, I'se e'en proceed wi' my tale. Ye see I hae been thinking it wad be a sair thing on twa young folk, like Grace and me, to put aff our marriage for mony years till I was abroad and came back again wi' some gear; and they say folk maunna take booty in the wars as they did lang syne, and the queen's pay is a sma' matter; there's nae gathering gear on that--and then my grandame's auld-- and my sisters wad sit peengin' at the ingle-side for want o' me to ding them about--and Earnscliff, or the neighbourhood, or maybe your ainsell, Elshie, might want some good turn that Hob Elliot could do ye--and it's a pity that the auld house o' the Heugh-foot should be wrecked a'thegither. Sae I was thinking--but deil hae me, that I should say sae," continued he, checking himself, "if I can bring mysell to ask a favour of ane that winna sae muckle as ware a word on me, to tell me if he hears me speaking till him."

"Say what thou wilt--do what thou wilt," answered the Dwarf from his cabin, "but begone, and leave me at peace."

"Weel, weel," replied Elliot, "since ye are willing to hear me, I'se make my tale short. Since ye are sae kind as to say ye are content to lend me as muckle siller as will stock and plenish the Heugh-foot, I am content, on my part, to accept the courtesy wi' mony kind thanks; and troth, I think it will be as safe in my hands as yours, if ye leave it flung about in that gate for the first loon body to lift, forbye the risk o' bad neighbours that can win through steekit doors and lockfast places, as I can tell to my cost. I say, since ye hae sae muckle consideration for me, I'se be blithe to accept your kindness; and my mother and me (she's a life-renter, and I am fiar, o' the lands o' Wideopen) would grant you a wadset, or an heritable bond, for the siller, and to pay the annual rent half-yearly; and Saunders Wyliecoat to draw the bond, and you to be at nae charge wi' the writings."

"Cut short thy jargon, and begone," said the Dwarf; "thy loquacious bull-headed honesty makes thee a more intolerable plague than the light-fingered courtier who would take a man's all without troubling him with either thanks, explanation, or apology. Hence, I say! thou art one of those tame slaves whose word is as good as their bond. Keep the money, principal and interest, until I demand it of thee."

"But," continued the pertinacious Borderer, "we are a' life-like and death-like, Elshie, and there really should be some black and white on this transaction. Sae just make me a minute, or missive, in ony form ye like, and I'se write it fair ower, and subscribe it before famous witnesses. Only, Elshie, I wad wuss ye to pit naething in't that may be prejudicial to my salvation; for I'll hae the minister to read it ower, and it wad only be exposing yoursell to nae purpose. And now I'm ganging awa', for ye'll be wearied o' my cracks, and I am wearied wi' cracking without an answer--and I'se bring ye a bit o' bride's-cake ane o' thae days, and maybe bring Grace to see you. Ye wad like to see Grace, man, for as dour as ye are--Eh, Lord I I wish he may be weel, that was a sair grane! or, maybe, he thought I was speaking of heavenly grace, and no of Grace Armstrong. Poor man, I am very doubtfu' o' his condition; but I am sure he is as kind to me as if I were his son, and a queer-looking father I wad hae had, if that had been e'en sae."

Hobbie now relieved his benefactor of his presence, and rode blithely home to display his treasure, and consult upon the means of repairing the damage which his fortune had sustained through the aggression of the Red Reiver of Westburnflat.

CHAPTER XI.

Three ruffians seized me yester morn, Alas! a maiden most forlorn;
They choked my cries with wicked might, And bound me on a
palfrey white: As sure as Heaven shall pity me, I cannot tell what
men they be. CHRISTABELLE.

The course of our story must here revert a little, to detail the
circumstances which had placed Miss Vere in the unpleasant
situation from which she was unexpectedly, and indeed
unintentionally liberated, by the appearance of Earnscliff and Elliot,
with their friends and followers, before the Tower of Westburnflat.

On the morning preceding the night in which Hobbie's house was
plundered and burnt, Miss Vere was requested by her father to
accompany him in a walk through a distant part of the romantic
grounds which lay round his castle of Ellieslaw. "To hear was to
obey," in the true style of Oriental despotism; but Isabella trembled
in silence while she followed her father through rough paths, now
winding by the side of the river, now ascending the cliffs which
serve for its banks. A single servant, selected perhaps for his
stupidity, was the only person who attended them. From her father's
silence, Isabella little doubted that he had chosen this distant and
sequestered scene to resume the argument which they had so
frequently maintained upon the subject of Sir Frederick's addresses,
and that he was meditating in what manner he should most
effectually impress upon her the necessity of receiving him as her
suitor. But her fears seemed for some time to be unfounded. The
only sentences which her father from time to time addressed to her,
respected the beauties of the romantic landscape through which they
strolled, and which varied its features at every step. To these
observations, although they seemed to come from a heart occupied
by more gloomy as well as more important cares, Isabella
endeavoured to answer in a manner as free and unconstrained as it
was possible for her to assume, amid the involuntary apprehensions
which crowded upon her imagination.

Sustaining with mutual difficulty a desultory conversation, they at
length gained the centre of a small wood, composed of large oaks,
intermingled with birches, mountain-ashes, hazel, holly, and a
variety of underwood. The boughs of the tall trees met closely above,
and the underwood filled up each interval between their trunks
below. The spot on which they stood was rather more open; still,

however, embowered under the natural arcade of tall trees, and darkened on the sides for a space around by a great and lively growth of copse-wood and bushes.

"And here, Isabella," said Mr. Vere, as he pursued the conversation, so often resumed, so often dropped, "here I would erect an altar to Friendship."

"To Friendship, sir!" said Miss Vere; "and why on this gloomy and sequestered spot, rather than elsewhere?"

"O, the propriety of the LOCALE is easily vindicated," replied her father, with a sneer. "You know, Miss Vere (for you, I am well aware, are a learned young lady), you know, that the Romans were not satisfied with embodying, for the purpose of worship, each useful quality and moral virtue to which they could give a name; but they, moreover, worshipped the same under each variety of titles and attributes which could give a distinct shade, or individual character, to the virtue in question. Now, for example, the Friendship to whom a temple should be here dedicated, is not Masculine Friendship, which abhors and despises duplicity, art, and disguise; but Female Friendship, which consists in little else than a mutual disposition on the part of the friends, as they call themselves, to abet each other in obscure fraud and petty intrigue."

"You are severe, sir," said Miss Vere.

"Only just," said her father; "a humble copier I am from nature, with the advantage of contemplating two such excellent studies as Lucy Ilderton and yourself."

"If I have been unfortunate enough to offend, sir, I can conscientiously excuse Miss Ilderton from being either my counsellor or confidante."

"Indeed! how came you, then," said Mr. Vere, "by the flippancy of speech, and pertness of argument, by which you have disgusted Sir Frederick, and given me of late such deep offence?"

"If my manner has been so unfortunate as to displease you, sir, it is impossible for me to apologize too deeply, or too sincerely; but I cannot confess the same contrition for having answered Sir Frederick flippantly when he pressed me rudely. Since he forgot I was a lady, it was time to show him that I am at least a woman."

"Reserve, then, your pertness for those who press you on the topic, Isabella," said her father coldly; "for my part, I am weary of the subject, and will never speak upon it again."

"God bless you, my dear father," said Isabella, seizing his reluctant hand "there is nothing you can impose on me, save the task of listening to this man's persecution, that I will call, or think, a hardship."

"You are very obliging, Miss Vere, when it happens to suit you to be dutiful," said her unrelenting father, forcing himself at the same time from the affectionate grasp of her hand; "but henceforward, child, I shall save myself the trouble of offering you unpleasant advice on any topic. You must look to yourself."

At this moment four ruffians rushed upon them. Mr. Vere and his servant drew their hangers, which it was the fashion of the time to wear, and attempted to defend themselves and protect Isabella. But while each of them was engaged by an antagonist, she was forced into the thicket by the two remaining villains, who placed her and themselves on horses which stood ready behind the copse- wood. They mounted at the same time, and, placing her between them, set of at a round gallop, holding the reins of her horse on each side. By many an obscure and winding path, over dale and down, through moss and moor, she was conveyed to the tower of Westburnflat, where she remained strictly watched, but not otherwise ill-treated, under the guardianship of the old woman, to whose son that retreat belonged. No entreaties could prevail upon the hag to give Miss Vere any information on the object of her being carried forcibly off, and confined in this secluded place. The arrival of Earnscliff, with a strong party of horsemen, before the tower, alarmed the robber. As he had already directed Grace Armstrong to be restored to her friends, it did not occur to him that this unwelcome visit was on her account; and seeing at the head of the party, Earnscliff, whose attachment to Miss Vere was whispered in the country, he doubted not that her liberation was the sole object of the attack upon his fastness. The dread of personal consequences compelled him to deliver up his prisoner in the manner we have already related.

At the moment the tramp of horses was heard which carried off the daughter of Ellieslaw, her father fell to the earth, and his servant, a stout young fellow, who was gaining ground on the ruffian with whom he had been engaged, left the combat to come to his master's assistance, little doubting that he had received a mortal wound, Both the villains immediately desisted from farther combat, and, retreating into the thicket, mounted their horses, and went off at full speed after their companions. Meantime, Dixon had the satisfaction to find Mr. Vere not only alive, but unwounded. He had overreached himself, and stumbled, it seemed, over the root of a tree, in making too eager a blow at his antagonist. The despair he felt at his daughter's disappearance, was, in Dixon's phrase, such as would have melted the heart of a whin stane, and he was so much exhausted by his feelings, and the vain researches which he made to discover the track of the ravishers, that a considerable time elapsed ere he reached home, and communicated the alarm to his domestics.

All his conduct and gestures were those of a desperate man.

"Speak not to me, Sir Frederick," he said impatiently; "You are no father--she was my child, an ungrateful one! I fear, but still my child--my only child. Where is Miss Ilderton? she must know something of this. It corresponds with what I was informed of her schemes. Go, Dixon, call Ratcliffe here Let him come without a minute's delay." The person he had named at this moment entered the room.

"I say, Dixon," continued Mr. Vere, in an altered tone, "let Mr. Ratcliffe know, I beg the favour of his company on particular business.--Ah! my dear sir," he proceeded, as if noticing him for the first time, "you are the very man whose advice can be of the utmost service to me in this cruel extremity."

"What has happened, Mr. Vere, to discompose you?" said Mr, Ratcliffe, gravely; and while the Laird of Ellieslaw details to him, with the most animated gestures of grief and indignation, the singular adventure of the morning, we shall take the opportunity to inform our readers of the relative circumstances in which these gentlemen stood to each other.

In early youth, Mr. Vere of Ellieslaw had been remarkable for a career of dissipation, which, in advanced life, he had exchanged for the no less destructive career of dark and turbulent ambition. In both cases, he had gratified the predominant passion without respect to the diminution of his private fortune, although, where such inducements were wanting, he was deemed close, avaricious, and grasping. His affairs being much embarrassed by his earlier extravagance, he went to England, where he was understood to have formed a very advantageous matrimonial connexion. He was many years absent from his family estate. Suddenly and unexpectedly he returned a widower, bringing with him his daughter, then a girl of about ten years old. From this moment his expense seemed unbounded, in the eyes of the simple inhabitants of his native mountains. It was supposed he must necessarily have plunged himself deeply in debt. Yet he continued to live in the same lavish expense, until some months before the commencement of our narrative, when the public opinion of his embarrassed circumstances was confirmed, by the residence of Mr. Ratcliffe at Ellieslaw Castle, who, by the tacit consent, though obviously to the great displeasure, of the lord of the mansion, seemed, from the moment of his arrival, to assume and exercise a predominant and unaccountable influence in the management of his private affairs.

Mr. Ratcliffe was a grave, steady, reserved man, in an advanced period of life. To those with whom he had occasion to speak upon business, he appeared uncommonly well versed in all its forms. With others he held little communication; but in any casual intercourse, or conversation, displayed the powers of an active and well-informed mind. For some time before taking up his final residence at the castle, he had been an occasional visitor there, and was at such times treated by Mr. Vere (contrary to his general practice towards those who were inferior to him in rank) with marked attention, and even deference. Yet his arrival always appeared to be an embarrassment to his host, and his departure a relief; so that, when he became a constant inmate of the family, it was impossible not to observe indications of the displeasure with which Mr. Vere regarded his presence. Indeed, their intercourse formed a singular mixture of confidence and constraint. Mr. Vere's most important affairs were regulated by Mr. Ratcliffe; and although he was none of those indulgent men of fortune, who, too indolent to manage their own business, are glad to devolve it upon another, yet, in many instances, he was observed to give up his own judgment, and submit to the contrary opinions which Mr. Ratcliffe did not hesitate distinctly to express.

Nothing seemed to vex Mr. Vere more than when strangers indicated any observation of the state of tutelage under which he appeared to labour. When it was noticed by Sir Frederick, or any of his intimates, he sometimes repelled their remarks haughtily and indignantly, and sometimes endeavoured to evade them, by saying, with a forced laugh, "That Ratcliffe knew his own importance, but that he was the most honest and skilful fellow in the world; and that it would be impossible for him to manage his English affairs without his advice and assistance." Such was the person who entered the room at the moment Mr. Vere was summoning him to his presence, and who now heard with surprise, mingled with obvious incredulity, the hasty narrative of what had befallen Isabella.

Her father concluded, addressing Sir Frederick and the other gentlemen, who stood around in astonishment, "And now, my friends, you see the most unhappy father in Scotland. Lend me your assistance, gentlemen--give me your advice, Mr. Ratcliffe. I am incapable of acting, or thinking, under the unexpected violence of such a blow."

"Let us take our horses, call our attendants, and scour the country in pursuit of the villains," said Sir Frederick.

"Is there no one whom you can suspect," said Ratcliffe, gravely, "of having some motive for this strange crime? These are not the days of romance, when ladies are carried off merely for their beauty."

"I fear," said Mr. Vere, "I can too well account for this strange incident. Read this letter, which Miss Lucy Ilderton thought fit to address from my house of Ellieslaw to young Mr. Earnscliff; whom, of all men, I have a hereditary right to call my enemy. You see she writes to him as the confidant of a passion which he has the assurance to entertain for my daughter; tells him she serves his cause with her friend very ardently, but that he has a friend in the garrison who serves him yet more effectually. Look particularly at the pencilled passages, Mr. Ratcliffe, where this meddling girl recommends bold measures, with an assurance that his suit would be successful anywhere beyond the bounds of the barony of Ellieslaw."

"And you argue, from this romantic letter of a very romantic young lady, Mr. Vere," said Ratcliffe, "that young Earnscliff has carried off your daughter, and committed a very great and criminal act of violence, on no better advice and assurance than that of Miss Lucy Ilderton?"

"What else can I think?" said Ellieslaw.

"What else CAN you think?" said Sir Frederick; "or who else could have any motive for committing such a crime?"

"Were that the best mode of fixing the guilt," said Mr. Ratcliffe, calmly, "there might easily be pointed out persons to whom such actions are more congenial, and who have also sufficient motives of instigation. Supposing it were judged advisable to remove Miss Vere to some place in which constraint might be exercised upon her inclinations to a degree which cannot at present be attempted under the roof of Ellieslaw Castle--What says Sir Frederick Langley to that supposition?"

"I say," returned Sir Frederick, "that although Mr. Vere may choose to endure in Mr. Ratcliffe freedoms totally inconsistent with his situation in life, I will not permit such license of innuendo, by word or look, to be extended to me, with impunity."

"And I say," said young Mareschal of Mareschal-Wells, who was also a guest at the castle, "that you are all stark mad to be standing wrangling here, instead of going in pursuit of the ruffians."

"I have ordered off the domestics already in the track most likely to overtake them," said Mr. Vere "if you will favour me with your company, we will follow them, and assist in the search."

The efforts of the party were totally unsuccessful, probably because Ellieslaw directed the pursuit to proceed in the direction of Earnscliff Tower, under the supposition that the owner would prove to be the author of the violence, so that they followed a direction diametrically opposite to that in which the ruffians had actually proceeded. In the evening they returned, harassed and out of spirits. But other guests had, in the meanwhile, arrived at the castle; and, after the recent loss sustained by the owner had been related, wondered at, and lamented, the recollection of it was, for the present, drowned in the discussion of deep political intrigues, of which the crisis and explosion were momentarily looked for.

Several of the gentlemen who took part in this divan were Catholics, and all of them stanch Jacobites, whose hopes were at present at the highest pitch, as an invasion, in favour of the Pretender, was daily expected from France, which Scotland, between the defenceless state of its garrisons and fortified places, and the general disaffection of the inhabitants, was rather prepared to welcome than to resist. Ratcliffe, who neither sought to assist at their consultations on this subject, nor was invited to do so, had, in the meanwhile, retired to his own apartment. Miss Ilderton was sequestered from society in a sort of honourable confinement, "until," said Mr. Vere, "she should be safely conveyed home to her father's house," an opportunity for which occurred on the following day.

The domestics could not help thinking it remarkable how soon the loss of Miss Vere, and the strange manner in which it had happened, seemed to be forgotten by the other guests at the castle. They knew not, that those the most interested in her fate were well acquainted with the cause of her being carried off, and the place of her retreat; and that the others, in the anxious and doubtful moments which preceded the breaking forth of a conspiracy, were little accessible to any feelings but what arose immediately out of their own machinations.

CHAPTER XII.

Some one way, some another--Do you know Where we may apprehend her?

The researches after Miss Vere were (for the sake of appearances, perhaps) resumed on the succeeding day, with similar bad success, and the party were returning towards Ellieslaw in the evening.

"It is singular," said Mareschal to Ratcliffe, "that four horsemen and a female prisoner should have passed through the country without leaving the slightest trace of their passage. One would think they had traversed the air, or sunk through the ground."

"Men may often," answered Ratcliffe, "arrive at the knowledge of that which is, from discovering that which is not. We have now scoured every road, path, and track leading from the castle, in all the various points of the compass, saving only that intricate and difficult pass which leads southward down the Westburn, and through the morasses."

"And why have we not examined that?" said Mareschal.

"O, Mr. Vere can best answer that question," replied his companion, dryly.

"Then I will ask it instantly," said Mareschal; and, addressing Mr. Vere, "I am informed, sir," said he, "there is a path we have not examined, leading by Westburnflat."

"O," said Sir Frederick, laughing, "we know the owner of Westburnflat well--a wild lad, that knows little difference between his neighbour's goods and his own; but, withal, very honest to his principles: he would disturb nothing belonging to Ellieslaw."

"Besides," said Mr. Vere, smiling mysteriously, "he had other tow on his distaff last night. Have you not heard young Elliot of the Heugh-foot has had his house burnt, and his cattle driven away, because he refused to give up his arms to some honest men that think of starting for the king?"

The company smiled upon each other, as at hearing of an exploit which favoured their own views.

"Yet, nevertheless," resumed Mareschal, "I think we ought to ride in this direction also, otherwise we shall certainly be blamed for our negligence."

No reasonable objection could be offered to this proposal, and the party turned their horses' heads towards Westburnflat.

They had not proceeded very far in that direction when the trampling of horses was heard, and a small body of riders were perceived advancing to meet them.

"There comes Earnscliff," said Mareschal; "I know his bright bay with the star in his front."

"And there is my daughter along with him," exclaimed Vere, furiously. "Who shall call my suspicions false or injurious now? Gentlemen--friends--lend me the assistance of your swords for the recovery of my child."

He unsheathed his weapon, and was imitated by Sir Frederick and several of the party, who prepared to charge those that were advancing towards them. But the greater part hesitated.

"They come to us in all peace and security," said Mareschal- Wells; "let us first hear what account they give us of this mysterious affair. If Miss Vere has sustained the slightest insult or injury from Earnscliff, I will be first to revenge her; but let us hear what they say."

"You do me wrong by your suspicions, Mareschal," continued Vere; "you are the last I would have expected to hear express them."

"You injure yourself, Ellieslaw, by your violence, though the cause may excuse it."

He then advanced a little before the rest, and called out, with a loud voice,--"Stand, Mr. Earnscliff; or do you and Miss Vere advance alone to meet us. You are charged with having carried that lady off from her father's house; and we are here in arms to shed our best blood for her recovery, and for bringing to justice those who have injured her."

"And who would do that more willingly than I, Mr. Mareschal?" said Earnscliff, haughtily,--"than I, who had the satisfaction this morning to liberate her from the dungeon in which I found her confined, and who am now escorting her back to the Castle of Ellieslaw?"

"Is this so, Miss Vere?" said Mareschal.

"It is," answered Isabella, eagerly,--"it is so; for Heaven's sake sheathe your swords. I will swear by all that is sacred, that I was carried off by ruffians, whose persons and object were alike unknown to me, and am now restored to freedom by means of this gentleman's gallant interference."

"By whom, and wherefore, could this have been done?" pursued Mareschal.--"Had you no knowledge of the place to which you were conveyed?--Earnscliff, where did you find this lady?"

But ere either question could be answered, Ellieslaw advanced, and, returning his sword to the scabbard, cut short the conference.

"When I know," he said, "exactly how much I owe to Mr. Earnscliff, he may rely on suitable acknowledgments; meantime," taking the bridle of Miss Vere's horse, "thus far I thank him for replacing my daughter in the power of her natural guardian."

A sullen bend of the head was returned by Earnscliff with equal haughtiness; and Ellieslaw, turning back with his daughter upon the road to his own house, appeared engaged with her in a conference so earnest, that the rest of the company judged it improper to intrude by approaching them too nearly. In the meantime, Earnscliff, as he took leave of the other gentlemen belonging to Ellieslaw's party, said aloud, "Although I am unconscious of any circumstance in my conduct that can authorize such a suspicion, I cannot but observe, that Mr. Vere seems to believe that I have had some hand in the atrocious violence which has been offered to his daughter. I request you, gentlemen, to take notice of my explicit denial of a charge so dishonourable; and that, although I can pardon the bewildering feelings of a father in such a moment, yet, if any other gentleman" (he looked hard at Sir Frederick Langley) "thinks my word and that of Miss Vere, with the evidence of my friends who accompany me, too slight for my exculpation, I will be happy--most happy--to repel the charge, as becomes a man who counts his honour dearer than his life."

"And I'll be his second," said Simon of Hackburn, "and take up ony twa o' ye, gentle or semple, laird or loon; it's a' ane to Simon."

"Who is that rough-looking fellow?" said Sir Frederick Langley, "and what has he to do with the quarrels of gentlemen?"

"I'se be a lad frae the Hie Te'iot," said Simon, "and I'se quarrel wi' ony body I like, except the king, or the laird I live under."

"Come," said; Mareschal, "let us have no brawls.--Mr. Earnscliff; although we do not think alike in some things, I trust we may be opponents, even enemies, if fortune will have it so, without losing our respect for birth, fair-play, and each other. I believe you as innocent of this matter as I am myself; and I will pledge myself that my cousin Ellieslaw, as soon as the perplexity attending these sudden events has left his judgment to its free exercise, shall handsomely acknowledge the very important service you have this day rendered him."

"To have served your cousin is a sufficient reward in itself-- Good evening, gentlemen," continued Earnscliff; "I see most of your party are already on their way to Ellieslaw."

Then saluting Mareschal with courtesy, and the rest of the party with indifference, Earnscliff turned his horse and rode towards the Heugh-foot, to concert measures with Hobbie Elliot for farther researches after his bride, of whose restoration to her friends he was still ignorant.

"There he goes," said Mareschal; "he is a fine, gallant young fellow, upon my soul; and yet I should like well to have a thrust with him on the green turf. I was reckoned at college nearly his equal with the foils, and I should like to try him at sharps."

"In my opinion," answered Sir Frederick Langley, "we have done very ill in having suffered him, and those men who are with him, to go off without taking away their arms; for the Whigs are very likely to draw to a head under such a sprightly young fellow as that."

"For shame, Sir Frederick!" exclaimed Mareschal; "do you think that Ellieslaw could, in honour, consent to any violence being offered to Earnscliff; when he entered his bounds only to bring back his daughter? or, if he were to be of your opinion, do you think that I, and the rest of these gentlemen, would disgrace ourselves by assisting in such a transaction? No, no, fair play and auld Scotland for ever! When the sword is drawn, I will be as ready to use it as any man; but while it is in the sheath, let us behave like gentlemen and neighbours."

Soon after this colloquy they reached the castle, when Ellieslaw, who had been arrived a few minutes before, met them in the court- yard.

"How is Miss Vere? and have you learned the cause of her being carried off?" asked Mareschal hastily.

"She is retired to her apartment greatly fatigued; and I cannot expect much light upon her adventure till her spirits are somewhat recruited," replied her father. "She and I were not the less obliged to you, Mareschal, and to my other friends, for their kind enquiries. But I must suppress the father's feelings for a while to give myself up to those of the patriot. You know this is the day fixed for our final decision--time presses--our friends are arriving, and I have opened house, not only for the gentry, but for the under spur-leathers whom we must necessarily employ. We have, therefore, little time to prepare to meet them.--Look over these lists, Marchie (an abbreviation by which Mareschal-Wells was known among his friends). Do you, Sir Frederick, read these letters from Lothian and the west--all is ripe for the sickle, and we have but to summon out the reapers."

"With all my heart," said Mareschal; "the more mischief the better sport."

Sir Frederick looked grave and disconcerted.

"Walk aside with me, my good friend," said Ellieslaw to the sombre baronet; "I have something for your private ear, with which I know you will be gratified."

They walked into the house, leaving Ratcliffe and Mareschal standing together in the court.

"And so," said Ratcliffe, "the gentlemen of your political persuasion think the downfall of this government so certain, that they disdain even to throw a decent disguise over the machinations of their party?"

"Faith, Mr. Ratcliffe," answered Mareschal, "the actions and sentiments YOUR friends may require to be veiled, but I am better pleased that ours can go barefaced."

"And is it possible," continued Ratcliffe, "that you, who, notwithstanding pour thoughtlessness and heat of temper (I beg pardon, Mr. Mareschal, I am a plain man)--that you, who, notwithstanding these constitutional defects, possess natural good sense and acquired information, should be infatuated enough to embroil yourself in such desperate proceedings? How does your head feel when you are engaged in these dangerous conferences?"

"Not quite so secure on my shoulders," answered Mareschal, "as if I were talking of hunting and hawking. I am not of so indifferent a mould as my cousin Ellieslaw, who speaks treason as if it were a child's nursery rhymes, and loses and recovers that sweet girl, his daughter, with a good deal less emotion on both occasions, than would have affected me had I lost and recovered a greyhound puppy. My temper is not quite so inflexible, nor my hate against government so inveterate, as to blind me to the full danger of the attempt."

"Then why involve yourself in it?" said Ratcliffe.

"Why, I love this poor exiled king with all my heart; and my father was an old Killiecrankie man, and I long to see some amends on the Unionist courtiers, that have bought and sold old Scotland, whose crown has been so long independent."

"And for the sake of these shadows," said his monitor, "you are going to involve your country in war and yourself in trouble?"

"I involve? No!--but, trouble for trouble, I had rather it came to-morrow than a month hence. COME, I know it will; and, as your country folks say, better soon than syne--it will never find me younger--and as for hanging, as Sir John Falstaff says, I can become a gallows as well as another. You know the end of the old ballad;

"Sae dauntonly, sae wantonly, Sae rantingly gaed he, He play'd a spring, and danced a round, Beneath the gallows tree."

"Mr. Mareschal, I am sorry for you," said his grave adviser.

"I am obliged to you, Mr. Ratcliffe; but I would not have you judge of our enterprise by my way of vindicating it; there are wiser heads than mine at the work."

"Wiser heads than yours may lie as low," said Ratcliffe, in a warning tone.

"Perhaps so; but no lighter heart shall; and, to prevent it being made heavier by your remonstrances, I will bid you adieu, Mr. Ratcliffe, till dinner-time, when you shall see that my apprehensions have not spoiled my appetite."

CHAPTER XIII.

To face the garment of rebellion With some fine colour, that may
please the eye Of fickle changelings, and poor discontents, Which
gape and rub the elbow at the news Of hurlyburly innovation.
HENRY THE FOURTH, PART II.

There had been great preparations made at Ellieslaw Castle for the
entertainment on this important day, when not only the gentlemen
of note in the neighbourhood, attached to the Jacobite interest, were
expected to rendezvous, but also many subordinate malecontents,
whom difficulty of circumstances, love of change, resentment against
England, or any of the numerous causes which inflamed men's
passions at the time, rendered apt to join in perilous enterprise. The
men of rank and substance were not many in number; for almost all
the large proprietors stood aloof, and most of the smaller gentry and
yeomanry were of the Presbyterian persuasion, and therefore,
however displeased with the Union, unwilling to engage in a
Jacobite conspiracy. But there were some gentlemen of property,
who, either from early principle, from religious motives, or sharing
the ambitious views of Ellieslaw, had given countenance to his
scheme; and there were, also, some fiery young men, like Mareschal,
desirous of signalizing themselves by engaging in a dangerous
enterprise, by which they hoped to vindicate the independence of
their country. The other members of the party were persons of
inferior rank and desperate fortunes, who were now ready to rise in
that part of the country, as they did afterwards in the year 1715,
under Forster and Derwentwater, when a troop, commanded by a
Border gentleman, named Douglas, consisted almost entirely of
freebooters, among whom the notorious Luck-in-a-bag, as he was
called, held a distinguished command. We think it necessary to
mention these particulars, applicable solely to the province in which
our scene lies; because, unquestionably, the Jacobite party, in the
other parts of the kingdom, consisted of much more formidable, as
well as much more respectable, materials.

One long table extended itself down the ample hall of Ellieslaw
Castle, which was still left much in the state in which it had been one
hundred years before, stretching, that is, in gloomy length, along the
whole side of the castle, vaulted with ribbed arches of freestone, the
groins of which sprung from projecting figures, that, carved into all
the wild forms which the fantastic imagination of a Gothic architect
could devise, grinned, frowned, and gnashed their tusks at the

assembly below. Long narrow windows lighted the banqueting room on both sides, filled up with stained glass, through which the sun emitted a dusky and discoloured light. A banner, which tradition averred to have been taken from the English at the battle of Sark, waved over the chair in which Ellieslaw presided, as if to inflame the courage of the guests, by reminding them of ancient victories over their neighbours. He himself, a portly figure, dressed on this occasion with uncommon care, and with features, which, though of a stern and sinister expression, might well be termed handsome, looked the old feudal baron extremely well. Sir Frederick Langley was placed on his right hand, and Mr. Mareschal of Mareschal-Wells on his left. Some gentlemen of consideration, with their sons, brothers, and nephews, were seated at the upper end of the table, and among these Mr. Ratcliffe had his place. Beneath the salt- cellar (a massive piece of plate which occupied the midst of the table) sate the SINE NOMINE TURBA, men whose vanity was gratified by holding even this subordinate space at the social board, while the distinction observed in ranking them was a salve to the pride of their superiors. That the lower house was not very select must be admitted, since Willie of Westburnflat was one of the party. The unabashed audacity of this fellow, in daring to present himself in the house of a gentleman, to whom he had just offered so flagrant an insult, can only be accounted for by supposing him conscious that his share in carrying off Miss Vere was a secret, safe in her possession and that of her father.

Before this numerous and miscellaneous party was placed a dinner, consisting, not indeed of the delicacies of the season, as the newspapers express it, but of viands, ample, solid, and sumptuous, under which the very board groaned. But the mirth was not in proportion to the good cheer. The lower end of the table were, for some time, chilled by constraint and respect on finding themselves members of so august an assembly; and those who were placed around it had those feelings of awe with which P. P., clerk of the parish, describes himself oppressed, when he first uplifted the psalm in presence of those persons of high worship, the wise Mr. Justice Freeman, the good Lady Jones, and the great Sir Thomas Truby. This ceremonious frost, however, soon gave way before the incentives to merriment, which were liberally supplied, and as liberally consumed by the guests of the lower description. They became talkative, loud, and even clamorous in their mirth.

But it was not in the power of wine or brandy to elevate the spirits of those who held the higher places at the banquet. They experienced the chilling revulsion of spirits which often takes place, when men are called upon to take a desperate resolution, after having placed themselves in circumstances where it is alike difficult to advance or to recede. The precipice looked deeper and more dangerous as they approached the brink, and each waited with an inward emotion of awe, expecting which of his confederates would set the example by plunging himself down. This inward sensation of fear and reluctance acted differently, according to the various habits and characters of the company. One looked grave; another looked silly; a third gazed with apprehension on the empty seats at the higher end of the table, designed for members of the conspiracy whose prudence had prevailed over their political zeal, and who had absented themselves from their consultations at this critical period; and some seemed to be reckoning up in their minds the comparative rank and prospects of those who were present and absent. Sir Frederick Langley was reserved, moody, and discontented. Ellieslaw himself made such forced efforts to raise the spirits of the company, as plainly marked the flagging of his own. Ratcliffe watched the scene with the composure of a vigilant but uninterested spectator. Mareschal alone, true to the thoughtless vivacity of his character, ate and drank, laughed and jested, and seemed even to find amusement in the embarrassment of the company.

"What has damped our noble courage this morning?" he exclaimed. "We seem to be met at a funeral, where the chief mourners must not speak above their breath, while the mutes and the saulies (looking to the lower end of the table) are carousing below. Ellieslaw, when will you LIFT? [To LIFT, meaning to lift the coffin, is the common expression for commencing a funeral.] where sleeps your spirit, man? and what has quelled the high hope of the Knight of Langley-dale?"

"You speak like a madman," said Ellieslaw; "do you not see how many are absent?"

"And what of that?" said Mareschal. "Did you not know before, that one-half of the world are better talkers than doers? For my part, I am much encouraged by seeing at least two-thirds of our friends true to the rendezvous, though I suspect one-half of these came to secure the dinner in case of the worst."

"There is no news from the coast which can amount to certainty of the King's arrival," said another of the company, in that tone of subdued and tremulous whisper which implies a failure of resolution.

"Not a line from the Earl of D--, nor a single gentleman from the southern side of the Border," said a third.

"Who is he that wishes for more men from England," exclaimed Mareschal, in a theatrical tone of affected heroism,

"My cousin Ellieslaw? No, my fair cousin, If we are doom'd to die--"

"For God's sake," said Ellieslaw, "spare us your folly at present, Mareschal."

"Well, then," said his kinsman, "I'll bestow my wisdom upon you instead, such as it is. If we have gone forward like fools, do not let us go back like cowards. We have done enough to draw upon us both the suspicion and vengeance of the government; do not let us give up before we have done something to deserve it. --What, will no one speak? Then I'll leap the ditch the first." And, starting up, he filled a beer-glass to the brim with claret, and waving his hand, commanded all to follow his example, and to rise up from their seats. All obeyed- the more qualified guests as if passively, the others with enthusiasm "Then, my friends, I give you the pledge of the day--The independence of Scotland, and the health of our lawful sovereign, King James the Eighth, now landed in Lothian, and, as I trust and believe, in full possession of his ancient capital!"

He quaffed off the wine, and threw the glass over his head.

"It should never," he said, "be profaned by a meaner toast."

All followed his example, and, amid the crash of glasses and the shouts of the company, pledged themselves to stand or fall with the principles and political interest which their toast expressed.

"You have leaped the ditch with a witness," said Ellieslaw, apart to Mareschal; "but I believe it is all for the best; at all events, we cannot now retreat from our undertaking. One man alone" (looking at Ratcliffe) "has refused the pledge; but of that by and by."

Then, rising up, he addressed the company in a style of inflammatory invective against the government and its measures, but especially the Union; a treaty, by means of which, he affirmed, Scotland had been at once cheated of her independence, her commerce, and her honour, and laid as a fettered slave at the foot of the rival against whom, through such a length of ages, through so many dangers, and by so much blood, she had honourably defended her rights. This was touching a theme which found a responsive chord in the bosom of every man present.

"Our commerce is destroyed," hollowed old John Rewcastle, a Jedburgh smuggler, from the lower end of the table.

"Our agriculture is ruined," said the Laird of Broken-girth-flow, a territory which, since the days of Adam, had borne nothing but ling and whortle-berries.

"Our religion is cut up, root and branch," said the pimple-nosed pastor of the Episcopal meeting-house at Kirkwhistle.

"We shall shortly neither dare shoot a deer nor kiss a wench, without a certificate from the presbytery and kirk-treasurer," said Mareschal-Wells.

"Or make a brandy jeroboam in a frosty morning, without license from a commissioner of excise," said the smuggler.

"Or ride over the fell in a moonless night," said Westburnflat, "without asking leave of young Earnscliff; or some Englified justice of the peace: thae were gude days on the Border when there was neither peace nor justice heard of."

"Let us remember our wrongs at Darien and Glencoe," continued Ellieslaw, "and take arms for the protection of our rights, our fortunes, our lives, and our families."

"Think upon genuine episcopal ordination, without which there can be no lawful clergy," said the divine.

"Think of the piracies committed on our East-Indian trade by Green and the English thieves," said William Willieson, half- owner and sole skipper of a brig that made four voyages annually between Cockpool and Whitehaven.

"Remember your liberties," rejoined Mareschal, who seemed to take a mischievous delight in precipitating the movements of the enthusiasm which he had excited, like a roguish boy, who, having lifted the sluice of a mill-dam, enjoys the clatter of the wheels which he has put in motion, without thinking of the mischief he may have occasioned. "Remember your liberties," he exclaimed; "confound cess, press, and presbytery, and the memory of old Willie that first brought them upon us!"

"Damn the gauger!" echoed old John Rewcastle; "I'll cleave him wi' my ain hand."

"And confound the country-keeper and the constable!" re-echoed Westburnflat; "I'll weize a brace of balls through them before morning."

"We are agreed, then," said Ellieslaw, when the shouts had somewhat subsided, "to bear this state of things no longer?"

"We are agreed to a man," answered his guests.

"Not literally so," said Mr. Ratcliffe; "for though I cannot hope to assuage the violent symptoms which seem so suddenly to have seized upon the company, yet I beg to observe, that so far as the opinion of a single member goes, I do not entirely coincide in the list of grievances which has been announced, and that I do utterly protest against the frantic measures which you seem disposed to adopt for removing them. I can easily suppose much of what has been spoken may have arisen out of the heat of the moment, or have been said perhaps in jest. But there are some jests of a nature very apt to transpire; and you ought to remember, gentlemen, that stone-walls have ears."

"Stone-walls may have ears," returned Ellieslaw, eyeing him with a look of triumphant malignity, "but domestic spies, Mr. Ratcliffe, will soon find themselves without any, if any such dares to continue his abode in a family where his coming was an unauthorized intrusion, where his conduct has been that of a presumptuous meddler, and from which his exit shall be that of a baffled knave, if he does not know how to take a hint."

"Mr. Vere," returned Ratcliffe, with calm contempt, "I am fully aware, that as soon as my presence becomes useless to you, which it must through the rash step you are about to adopt, it will immediately become unsafe to myself, as it has always been hateful to you. But I have one protection, and it is a strong one; for you would not willingly hear me detail before gentlemen, and men of honour, the singular circumstances in which our connexion took its rise. As to the rest, I rejoice at its conclusion; and as I think that Mr. Mareschal and some other gentlemen will guarantee the safety of my ears and of my throat (for which last I have more reason to be apprehensive) during the course of the night, I shall not leave your castle till to-morrow morning."

"Be it so, sir," replied Mr. Vere; "you are entirely safe from my resentment, because you are beneath it, and not because I am afraid of your disclosing my family secrets, although, for your own sake, I warn you to beware how you do so. Your agency and intermediation can be of little consequence to one who will win or lose all, as lawful right or unjust usurpation shall succeed in the struggle that is about to ensue. Farewell, sir."

Ratcliffe arose, and cast upon him a look, which Vere seemed to sustain with difficulty, and, bowing to those around him, left the room.

This conversation made an impression on many of the company, which Ellieslaw hastened to dispel, by entering upon the business of the day. Their hasty deliberations went to organize an immediate insurrection. Ellieslaw, Mareschal, and Sir Frederick Langley were chosen leaders, with powers to direct their farther measures. A place of rendezvous was appointed, at which all agreed to meet early on the ensuing day, with such followers and friends to the cause as each could collect around him. Several of the guests retired to make the necessary preparations; and Ellieslaw made a formal apology to the others, who, with Westburnflat and the old smuggler, continued to ply the bottle stanchly, for leaving the head of the table, as he must necessarily hold a separate and sober conference with the coadjutors whom they had associated with him in the command. The apology was the more readily accepted, as he prayed them, at the same time, to continue to amuse themselves with such refreshments as the cellars of the castle afforded. Shouts of applause followed their retreat; and the names of Vere, Langley, and, above all, of Mareschal, were thundered forth in chorus, and bathed with copious bumpers repeatedly, during the remainder of the evening.

When the principal conspirators had retired into a separate apartment, they gazed on each other for a minute with a sort of embarrassment, which, in Sir Frederick's dark features, amounted to an expression of discontented sullenness. Mareschal was the first to break the pause, saying, with a loud burst of laughter, --"Well! we are fairly embarked now, gentlemen--VOGUE LA GALERE!"

"We may thank you for the plunge," said Ellieslaw.

"Yes; but I don't know how far you will thank me," answered Mareschal, "when I show you this letter which I received just before we sat down. My servant told me it was delivered by a man he had never seen before, who went off at the gallop, after charging him to put it into my own hand."

Ellieslaw impatiently opened the letter, and read aloud--

EDINBURGH,--

HOND. SIR, Having obligations to your family, which shall be nameless, and learning that you are one of the company of, adventurers doing business for the house of James and Company, late merchants in London, now in Dunkirk, I think it right to send you this early and private information, that the vessels you expected have been driven off the coast, without having been able to break bulk, or to land any part of their cargo; and that the west-country partners have resolved to withdraw their name from the firm, as it must prove a losing concern. Having good hope you will avail yourself of this early information, to do what is needful for your own security, I rest your humble servant, NIHIL NAMELESS.

FOR RALPH MARESCHAL, OF MARESCHAL-WELLS --THESE WITH CARE AND SPEED.

Sir Frederick's jaw dropped, and his countenance blackened, as the letter was read, and Ellieslaw exclaimed,--"Why, this affects the very mainspring of our enterprise. If the French fleet, with the king on board, has been chased off by the English, as this d--d scrawl seems to intimate, where are we?"

"Just where we were this morning, I think," said Mareschal, still laughing.

"Pardon me, and a truce to your ill-timed mirth, Mr. Mareschal; this morning we were not committed publicly, as we now stand committed by your own mad act, when you had a letter in your pocket apprizing you that our undertaking was desperate."

"Ay, ay, I expected you would say so. But, in the first place, my friend Nihil Nameless and his letter may be all a flam; and, moreover, I would have you know that I am tired of a party that does nothing but form bold resolutions overnight, and sleep them away with their wine before morning. The government are now unprovided of men and ammunition; in a few weeks they will have enough of both: the country is now in a flame against them; in a few weeks, betwixt the effects of self-interest, of fear, and of lukewarm indifference, which are already so visible, this first fervour will be as cold as Christmas. So, as I was determined to go the vole, I have taken care you shall dip as deep as I; it signifies nothing plunging. You are fairly in the bog, and must struggle through."

"You are mistaken with respect to one of us, Mr. Mareschal," said Sir Frederick Langley; and, applying himself to the bell, he desired the person who entered to order his servants and horses instantly.

"You must not leave us, Sir Frederick," said Ellieslaw; it we have our musters to go over."

"I will go to-night, Mr. Vere," said Sir Frederick, "and write you my intentions in this matter when I am at home."

"Ay," said Mareschal, "and send them by a troop of horse from Carlisle to make us prisoners? Look ye, Sir Frederick, I for one will neither be deserted nor betrayed; and if you leave Ellieslaw Castle to-night, it shall be by passing over my dead body."

"For shame! Mareschal," said Mr. Vere, "how can you so hastily misinterpret our friend's intentions? I am sure Sir Frederick can only be jesting with us; for, were he not too honourable to dream of deserting the cause, he cannot but remember the full proofs we have of his accession to it, and his eager activity in advancing it. He cannot but be conscious, besides, that the first information will be readily received by government, and that if the question be, which can first lodge intelligence of the affair, we can easily save a few hours on him."

"You should say you, and not we, when you talk of priorities in such a race of treachery; for my part, I won't enter my horse for such a plate," said Mareschal; and added betwixit his teeth, "A pretty pair of fellows to trust a man's neck with!"

"I am not to be intimidated from doing what I think proper," said Sir Frederick Langley; "and my first step shall be to leave Ellieslaw. I have no reason to keep faith with one" (looking at Vere) "who has kept none with me."

"In what respect," said Ellieslaw, silencing, with a motion of his hand, his impetuous kinsman--"how have I disappointed you, Sir Frederick?"

"In the nearest and most tender point--you have trifled with me concerning our proposed alliance, which you well knew was the gage of our political undertaking. This carrying off and this bringing back of Miss Vere,--the cold reception I have met with from her, and the excuses with which you cover it, I believe to be mere evasions, that you may yourself retain possession of the estates which are hers by right, and make me, in the meanwhile, a tool in your desperate enterprise, by holding out hopes and expectations which you are resolved never to realize."

"Sir Frederick, I protest, by all that is sacred--"

"I will listen to no protestations; I have been cheated with them too long," answered Sir Frederick.

"If you leave us," said Ellieslaw, "you cannot but know both your ruin and ours is certain; all depends on our adhering together."

"Leave me to take care of myself," returned the knight; "but were what you say true, I would rather perish than be fooled any farther."

"Can nothing--no surety convince you of my sincerity?" said Ellieslaw, anxiously; "this morning I should have repelled your unjust suspicions as an insult; but situated as we now are--"

"You feel yourself compelled to be sincere?" retorted Sir Frederick. "If you would have me think so, there is but one way to convince me of it--let your daughter bestow her hand on me this evening."

"So soon?--impossible," answered Vere; "think of her late alarm-- of our present undertaking."

"I will listen to nothing but to her consent, plighted at the altar. You have a chapel in the castle--Doctor Hobbler is present among the company-this proof of your good faith to-night, and we are again joined in heart and hand. If you refuse me when it is so much for your advantage to consent, how shall I trust you to-morrow, when I shall stand committed in your undertaking, and unable to retract?"

"And I am to understand, that, if you can be made my son-in-law to-night, our friendship is renewed?" said Ellieslaw.

"Most infallibly, and most inviolably," replied Sir Frederick.

"Then," said Vere, "though what you ask is premature, indelicate, and unjust towards my character, yet, Sir Frederick, give me your hand--my daughter shall be your wife."

"This night?"

"This very night," replied Ellieslaw, "before the clock strikes twelve."

"With her own consent, I trust," said Mareschal; "for I promise you both, gentlemen, I will not stand tamely by, and see any violence put on the will of my pretty kinswoman."

"Another pest in this hot-headed fellow," muttered Ellieslaw; and then aloud, "With her own consent? For what do you take me, Mareschal, that you should suppose your interference necessary to protect my daughter against her father? Depend upon it, she has no repugnance to Sir Frederick Langley."

"Or rather to be called Lady Langley? faith, like enough--there are many women might be of her mind; and I beg your pardon, but these sudden demands and concessions alarmed me a little on her account."

"It is only the suddenness of the proposal that embarrasses me," said Ellieslaw; "but perhaps if she is found intractable, Sir Frederick will consider--"

"I will consider nothing, Mr. Vere--your daughter's hand to- night, or I depart, were it at midnight--there is my ultimatum."

"I embrace it," said Ellieslaw; "and I will leave you to talk upon our military preparations, while I go to prepare my daughter for so sudden a change of condition."

So saying, he left the company.

CHAPTER XIV.

He brings Earl Osmond to receive my vows. O dreadful change! for
Tancred, haughty Osmond. TANCRED AND SIGISMUNDA.

Mr. Vere, whom long practice of dissimulation had enabled to model
his very gait and footsteps to aid the purposes of deception, walked
along the stone passage, and up the first flight of steps towards Miss
Vere's apartment, with the alert, firm, and steady pace of one who is
bound, indeed, upon important business, but who entertains no
doubt he can terminate his affairs satisfactorily. But when out of
hearing of the gentlemen whom he had left, his step became so slow
and irresolute, as to correspond with his doubts and his fears. At
length he paused in an antechamber to collect his ideas, and form his
plan of argument, before approaching his daughter.

"In what more hopeless and inextricable dilemma was ever an
unfortunate man involved!" Such was the tenor of his reflections.--
"If we now fall to pieces by disunion, there can be little doubt that
the government will take my life as the prime agitator of the
insurrection. Or, grant I could stoop to save myself by a hasty
submission, am I not, even in that case, utterly ruined? I have broken
irreconcilably with Ratcliffe, and can have nothing to expect from
that quarter but insult and persecution. I must wander forth an
impoverished and dishonoured man, without even the means of
sustaining life, far less wealth sufficient to counterbalance the infamy
which my countrymen, both those whom I desert and those whom I
join, will attach to the name of the political renegade. It is not to be
thought of. And yet, what choice remains between this lot and the
ignominious scaffold? Nothing can save me but reconciliation with
these men; and, to accomplish this, I have promised to Langley that
Isabella shall marry him ere midnight, and to Mareschal, that she
shall do so without compulsion. I have but one remedy betwixt me
and ruin--her consent to take a suitor whom she dislikes, upon such
short notice as would disgust her, even were he a favoured lover --
But I must trust to the romantic generosity of her disposition; and let
me paint the necessity of her obedience ever so strongly, I cannot
overcharge its reality."

Having finished this sad chain of reflections upon his perilous
condition, he entered his daughter's apartment with every nerve
bent up to the support of the argument which he was about to
sustain. Though a deceitful and ambitious man, he was not so

devoid of natural affection but that he was shocked at the part he was about to act, in practising on the feelings of a dutiful and affectionate child; but the recollections, that, if he succeeded, his daughter would only be trepanned into an advantageous match, and that, if he failed, he himself was a lost man, were quite sufficient to drown all scruples.

He found Miss Vere seated by the window of her dressing-room, her head reclining on her hand, and either sunk in slumber, or so deeply engaged in meditation, that she did not hear the noise he made at his entrance. He approached with his features composed to a deep expression of sorrow and sympathy, and, sitting down beside her, solicited her attention by quietly taking her hand, a motion which he did not fail to accompany with a deep sigh.

"My father!" said Isabella, with a sort of start, which expressed at least as much fear, as joy or affection.

"Yes, Isabella," said Vere, "your unhappy father, who comes now as a penitent to crave forgiveness of his daughter for an injury done to her in the excess of his affection, and then to take leave of her for ever."

"Sir? Offence to me take leave for ever? What does all this mean?" said Miss Vere.

"Yes, Isabella, I am serious. But first let me ask you, have you no suspicion that I may have been privy to the strange chance which befell you yesterday morning?"

"You, sir?" answered Isabella, stammering between a consciousness that he had guessed her thoughts justly, and the shame as well as fear which forbade her to acknowledge a suspicion so degrading and so unnatural.

"Yes!" he continued, "your hesitation confesses that you entertained such an opinion, and I have now the painful task of acknowledging that your suspicions have done me no injustice. But listen to my motives. In an evil hour I countenanced the addresses of Sir Frederick Langley, conceiving it impossible that you could have any permanent objections to a match where the advantages were, in most respects, on your side. In a worse, I entered with him into measures calculated to restore our banished monarch, and the independence of my country. He has taken advantage of my unguarded confidence, and now has my life at his disposal."

"Your life, sir?" said Isabella, faintly.

"Yes, Isabella," continued her father, "the life of him who gave life to you. So soon as I foresaw the excesses into which his headlong passion (for, to do him justice, I believe his unreasonable conduct arises from excess of attachment to you) was likely to hurry him, I endeavoured, by finding a plausible pretext for your absence for some weeks, to extricate myself from the dilemma in which I am placed. For this purpose I wished, in case your objections to the match continued insurmountable, to have sent you privately for a few months to the convent of your maternal aunt at Paris. By a series of mistakes you have been brought from the place of secrecy and security which I had destined for your temporary abode. Fate has baffled my last chance of escape, and I have only to give you my blessing, and send you from the castle with Mr. Ratcliffe, who now leaves it; my own fate will soon be decided."

"Good Heaven, sir! can this be possible?" exclaimed Isabella. "O, why was I freed from the restraint in which you placed me? or why did you not impart your pleasure to me?"

"Think an instant, Isabella. Would you have had me prejudice in your opinion the friend I was most desirous of serving, by communicating to you the injurious eagerness with which he pursued his object? Could I do so honourably, having promised to assist his suit?--But it is all over, I and Mareschal have made up our minds to die like men; it only remains to send you from hence under a safe escort."

"Great powers! and is there no remedy?" said the terrified young woman.

"None, my child," answered Vere, gently, "unless one which you would not advise your father to adopt--to be the first to betray his friends."

"O, no! no!" she answered, abhorrently yet hastily, as if to reject the temptation which the alternative presented to her. "But is there no other hope--through flight--through mediation --through supplication?--I will bend my knee to Sir Frederick!"

"It would be a fruitless degradation; he is determined on his course, and I am equally resolved to stand the hazard of my fate. On one condition only he will turn aside from his purpose, and that condition my lips shall never utter to you."

"Name it, I conjure you, my dear father!" exclaimed Isabella. "What CAN he ask that we ought not to grant, to prevent the hideous catastrophe with which you are threatened?"

"That, Isabella," said Vere, solemnly, "you shall never know, until your father's head has rolled on the bloody scaffold; then, indeed, you will learn there was one sacrifice by which he might have been saved."

"And why not speak it now?" said Isabella; "do you fear I would flinch from the sacrifice of fortune for your preservation? or would you bequeath me the bitter legacy of life-long remorse, so oft as I shall think that you perished, while there remained one mode of preventing the dreadful misfortune that overhangs you?"

"Then, my child," said Vere, "since you press me to name what I would a thousand times rather leave in silence, I must inform you that he will accept for ransom nothing but your hand in marriage, and that conferred before midnight this very evening!"

"This evening, sir?" said the young lady, struck with horror at the proposal--"and to such a man!--A man?--a monster, who could wish to win the daughter by threatening the life of the father --it is impossible!"

"You say right, my child," answered her father, "it is indeed impossible; nor have I either the right or the wish to exact such a sacrifice--It is the course of nature that the old should die and be forgot, and the young should live and be happy."

"My father die, and his child can save him!--but no--no--my dear father, pardon me, it is impossible; you only wish to guide me to your wishes. I know your object is what you think my happiness, and this dreadful tale is only told to influence my conduct and subdue my scruples."

"My daughter," replied Ellieslaw, in a tone where offended authority seemed to struggle with parental affection, "my child suspects me of inventing a false tale to work upon her feelings! Even this I must bear, and even from this unworthy suspicion I must descend to vindicate myself. You know the stainless honour of your cousin Mareschal--mark what I shall write to him, and judge from his answer, if the danger in which we stand is not real, and whether I have not used every means to avert it."

He sate down, wrote a few lines hastily, and handed them to Isabella, who, after repeated and painful efforts, cleared her eyes and head sufficiently to discern their purport.

"Dear cousin," said the billet, "I find my daughter, as I expected, in despair at the untimely and premature urgency of Sir Frederick Langley. She cannot even comprehend the peril in which we stand, or how much we are in his power-- Use your influence with him, for Heaven's sake, to modify proposals, to the acceptance of which I cannot, and will not, urge my child against all her own feelings, as well as those of delicacy and propriety, and oblige your loving cousin,--R. V."

In the agitation of the moment, when her swimming eyes and dizzy brain could hardly comprehend the sense of what she looked upon, it is not surprising that Miss Vere should have omitted to remark that this letter seemed to rest her scruples rather upon the form and time of the proposed union, than on a rooted dislike to the suitor proposed to her. Mr. Vere rang the bell, and gave the letter to a servant to be delivered to Mr. Mareschal, and, rising from his chair, continued to traverse the apartment in silence and in great agitation until the answer was returned. He glanced it over, and wrung the hand of his daughter as he gave it to her. The tenor was as follows:--

"My dear kinsman, I have already urged the knight on the point you mention, and I find him as fixed as Cheviot. I am truly sorry my fair cousin should be pressed to give up any of her maidenly rights. Sir Frederick consents, however, to leave the castle with me the instant the ceremony is performed, and we will raise our followers and begin the fray. Thus there is great hope the bridegroom may be knocked on the head before he and the bride can meet again, so Bell has a fair chance to be Lady Langley A TRES BON MARCHE. For the rest, I can only say, that if she can make up her mind to the alliance at all--it is no time for mere maiden ceremony--my pretty cousin must needs consent to marry in haste, or we shall all repent at leisure, or rather have very little leisure to repent; which is all at present from him who rests your affectionate kinsman,--R. M."

"P.S.--Tell Isabella that I would rather cut the knight's throat after all, and end the dilemma that way, than see her constrained to marry him against her will."

When Isabella had read this letter, it dropped from her hand, and she would, at the same time, have fallen from her chair, had she not been supported by her father.

"My God, my child will die!" exclaimed Vere, the feelings of nature overcoming, even in HIS breast, the sentiments of selfish policy; "look up, Isabella--look up, my child--come what will, you shall not be the sacrifice--I will fall myself with the consciousness I leave you happy--My child may weep on my grave, but she shall not--not in this instance--reproach my memory." He called a servant.--"Go, bid Ratcliffe come hither directly."

During this interval, Miss Vere became deadly pale, clenched her hands, pressing the palms strongly together, closed her eyes, and drew her lips with strong compression, as if the severe constraint which she put upon her internal feelings extended even to her muscular organization. Then raising her head, and drawing in her breath strongly ere she spoke, she said, with firmness, --"Father, I consent to the marriage."

"You shall not--you shall not,--my child--my dear child--you shall not embrace certain misery to free me from uncertain danger."

So exclaimed Ellieslaw; and, strange and inconsistent beings that we are! he expressed the real though momentary feelings of his heart.

"Father," repeated Isabella, "I will consent to this marriage."

"No, my child, no--not now at least--we will humble ourselves to obtain delay from him; and yet, Isabella, could you overcome a dislike which has no real foundation, think, in other respects, what a match!--wealth--rank--importance."

"Father!" reiterated Isabella, "I have consented."

It seemed as if she had lost the power of saying anything else, or even of varying the phrase which, with such effort, she had compelled herself to utter.

"Heaven bless thee, my child!--Heaven bless thee!--And it WILL bless thee with riches, with pleasure, with power."

Miss Vere faintly entreated to be left by herself for the rest of the evening.

"But will you not receive Sir Frederick?" said her father, anxiously.

"I will meet him," she replied, "I will meet him--when I must, and where I must; but spare me now."

"Be it so, my dearest; you shall know no restraint that I can save you from. Do not think too hardly of Sir Frederick for this,--it is an excess of passion."

Isabella waved her hand impatiently.

"Forgive me, my child--I go--Heaven bless thee. At eleven--if you call me not before--at eleven I come to seek you."

"When he left Isabella she dropped upon her knees--"Heaven aid me to support the resolution I have taken-- Heaven only can--O, poor Earnscliff! who shall comfort him? and with what contempt will he pronounce her name, who listened to him to-day and gave herself to another at night! But let him despise me--better so than that he should know the truth--let him despise me; if it will but lessen his grief, I should feel comfort in the loss of his esteem."

She wept bitterly; attempting in vain, from time to time, to commence the prayer for which she had sunk on her knees, but unable to calm her spirits sufficiently for the exercise of devotion. As she remained in this agony of mind, the door of her apartment was slowly opened.

CHAPTER XV.

The darksome cave they enter, where they found The woful man, low sitting on the ground, Musing full sadly in his sullen mind. FAERY QUEEN.

The intruder on Miss Vere's sorrows was Ratcliffe. Ellieslaw had, in the agitation of his mind, forgotten to countermand the order he had given to call him thither, so that he opened the door with the words, "You sent for me, Mr. Vere." Then looking around--"Miss Vere, alone! on the ground! and in tears!"

"Leave me--leave me, Mr. Ratcliffe," said the unhappy young lady.

"I must not leave you," said Ratcliffe; "I have been repeatedly requesting admittance to take my leave of you, and have been refused, until your father himself sent for me. Blame me not, if I am bold and intrusive; I have a duty to discharge which makes me so."

"I cannot listen to you--I cannot speak to you, Mr. Ratcliffe; take my best wishes, and for God's sake leave me."

"Tell me only," said Ratcliffe, "is it true that this monstrous match is to go forward, and this very night? I heard the servants proclaim it as I was on the great staircase--I heard the directions given to clear out the chapel."

"Spare me, Mr. Ratcliffe," replied the luckless bride; "and from the state in which you see me, judge of the cruelty of these questions."

"Married? to Sir Frederick Langley? and this night? It must not cannot--shall not be."

"It MUST be, Mr. Ratcliff, or my father is ruined."

"Ah! I understand," answered Ratcliffe; "and you have sacrificed yourself to save him who--But let the virtue of the child atone for the faults of the father it is no time to rake them up.--What CAN be done? Time presses--I know but one remedy--with four-and- twenty hours I might find many--Miss Vere, you must implore the protection of the only human being who has it in his power to control the course of events which threatens to hurry you before it."

"And what human being," answered Miss Vere, "has such power?"

"Start not when I name him," said Ratcliffe, coming near her, and speaking in a low but distinct voice. "It is he who is called Elshender the Recluse of Mucklestane-Moor."

"You are mad, Mr. Ratcliffe, or you mean to insult my misery by an ill-timed jest!"

"I am as much in my senses, young lady," answered her adviser, "as you are; and I am no idle jester, far less with misery, least of all with your misery. I swear to you that this being (who is other far than what he seems) actually possesses the means of redeeming you from this hateful union."

"And of insuring my father's safety?"

"Yes! even that," said Ratcliffe, "if you plead his cause with him--yet how to obtain admittance to the Recluse!"

"Fear not that," said Miss Vere, suddenly recollecting the incident of the rose; "I remember he desired me to call upon him for aid in my extremity, and gave me this flower as a token. Ere it faded away entirely, I would need, he said, his assistance: is it possible his words can have been aught but the ravings of insanity?"

"Doubt it not fear it not--but above all," said Ratcliffe, "let us lose no time--are you at liberty, and unwatched?"

"I believe so," said Isabella: "but what would you have me to do?"

"Leave the castle instantly," said Ratcliffe, "and throw yourself at the feet of this extraordinary man, who in circumstances that seem to argue the extremity of the most contemptible poverty, possesses yet an almost absolute influence over your fate.-- Guests and servants are deep in their carouse--the leaders sitting in conclave on their treasonable schemes--my horse stands ready in the stable--I will saddle one for you, and meet you at the little garden-gate--O, let no doubt of my prudence or fidelity prevent your taking the only step in your power to escape the dreadful fate which must attend the wife of Sir Frederick Langley!"

"Mr. Ratcliffe," said Miss Vere, "you have always been esteemed a man of honour and probity, and a drowning wretch will always catch at the feeblest twig,--I will trust you--I will follow your advice--I will meet you at the garden-gate."

She bolted the outer-door of her apartment as soon as Mr. Ratcliffe left her, and descended to the garden by a separate stair of communication which opened to her dressing-room. On the way she felt inclined to retract the consent she had so hastily given to a plan so hopeless and extravagant. But as she passed in her descent a private door which entered into the chapel from the back-stair, she heard the voice of the female-servants as they were employed in the task of cleaning it.

"Married! and to sae bad a man--Ewhow, sirs! onything rather than that."

"They are right--they are right," said Miss Vere, "anything rather than that!"

She hurried to the garden. Mr. Ratcliffe was true to his appointment--the horses stood saddled at the garden-gate, and in a few minutes they were advancing rapidly towards the hut of the Solitary.

While the ground was favourable, the speed of their journey was such as to prevent much communication; but when a steep ascent compelled them to slacken their pace, a new cause of apprehension occurred to Miss Vere's mind.

"Mr. Ratcliffe," she said, pulling up her horse's bridle, "let us prosecute no farther a journey, which nothing but the extreme agitation of my mind can vindicate my having undertaken--I am well aware that this man passes among the vulgar as being possessed of supernatural powers, and carrying on an intercourse with beings of another world; but I would have you aware I am neither to be imposed on by such follies, nor, were I to believe in their existence, durst I, with my feelings of religion, apply to this being in my distress."

"I should have thought, Miss Vere," replied Ratcliffe, "my character and habits of thinking were so well known to you, that you might have held me exculpated from crediting in such absurdity."

"But in what other mode," said Isabella, "can a being, so miserable himself in appearance, possess the power of assisting me?"

"Miss Vere." said Ratcliffe, after a momentary pause, "I am bound by a solemn oath of secrecy--You must, without farther explanation, be satisfied with my pledged assurance, that he does possess the power, if you can inspire him with the will; and that, I doubt not, you will be able to do."

"Mr. Ratcliffe," said Miss Vere, "you may yourself be mistaken; you ask an unlimited degree of confidence from me."

"Recollect, Miss Vere," he replied, "that when, in your humanity, you asked me to interfere with your father in favour of Haswell and his ruined family--when you requested me to prevail on him to do a thing most abhorrent to his nature--to forgive an injury and remit a penalty--I stipulated that you should ask me no questions concerning the sources of my influence--You found no reason to distrust me then, do not distrust me now."

"But the extraordinary mode of life of this man," said Miss Vere; "his seclusion--his figure--the deepness of mis-anthropy which he is said to express in his language--Mr. Ratcliffe, what can I think of him if he really possesses the powers you ascribe to him?"

"This man, young lady, was bred a Catholic, a sect which affords a thousand instances of those who have retired from power and affluence to voluntary privations more strict even than his."

"But he avows no religious motive," replied Miss Vere.

"No," replied Ratcliffe; "disgust with the world has operated his retreat from it without assuming the veil of superstition. Thus far I may tell you--he was born to great wealth, which his parents designed should become greater by his union with a kinswoman, whom for that purpose they bred up in their own house. You have seen his figure; judge what the young lady must have thought of the lot to which she was destined--Yet, habituated to his appearance, she showed no reluctance, and the friends of--of the person whom I speak of, doubted not that the excess of his attachment, the various acquisitions of his mind, his many and amiable qualities, had overcome the natural horror which his destined bride must have entertained at an exterior so dreadfully inauspicious."

"And did they judge truly?" said Isabella.

"You shall hear. He, at least, was fully aware of his own deficiency; the sense of it haunted him like a phantom. 'I am,' was his own expression to me,--I mean to a man whom he trusted,-- 'I am, in spite of what you would say, a poor miserable outcast, fitter to have been smothered in the cradle than to have been brought up to scare the world in which I crawl.' The person whom he addressed in vain endeavoured to impress him with the indifference to external form which is the natural result of philosophy, or entreat him to recall the superiority of mental talents to the more attractive attributes that are merely personal. 'I hear you,' he would reply; 'but you speak the voice of cold-blooded stoicism, or, at least, of friendly partiality. But look at every book which we have read, those excepted of that abstract philosophy which feels no responsive voice in our natural feelings. Is not personal form, such as at least can be tolerated without horror and disgust, always represented as essential to our ideas of a friend, far more a lover? Is not such a mis-shapen monster as I am, excluded, by the very fiat of Nature, from her fairest enjoyments? What but my wealth prevents all--perhaps even Letitia, or you--from shunning me as something foreign to your nature, and more odious, by bearing that distorted resemblance to humanity which we observe in the animal tribes that are more hateful to man because they seem his caricature?'"

"You repeat the sentiments of a madman," said Miss Vere.

"No," replied her conductor, "unless a morbid and excessive sensibility on such a subject can be termed insanity. "Yet I will not deny that this governing feeling and apprehension carried the person who entertained it, to lengths which indicated a deranged imagination. He appeared to think that it was necessary for him, by exuberant, and not always well-chosen instances of liberality, and even profusion, to unite himself to the human race, from which he conceived himself naturally dissevered. The benefits which he bestowed, from a disposition naturally philanthropical in an uncommon degree, were exaggerated by the influence of the goading reflection, that more was necessary from him than from others,--lavishing his treasures as if to bribe mankind to receive him into their class. It is scarcely necessary to say, that the bounty which flowed from a source so capricious was often abused, and his confidence frequently betrayed. These disappointments, which occur to all, more or less, and most to such as confer benefits without just discrimination, his diseased fancy set down to the hatred and contempt excited by his personal deformity.-- But I fatigue you, Miss Vere?"

"No, by no means; I--I could not prevent my attention from wandering an instant; pray proceed."

"He became at length," continued Ratcliffe, "the most ingenious self-tormentor of whom I have ever heard; the scoff of the rabble, and the sneer of the yet more brutal vulgar of his own rank, was to him agony and breaking on the wheel. He regarded the laugh of the common people whom he passed on the street, and the suppressed titter, or yet more offensive terror, of the young girls to whom he was introduced in company, as proofs of the true sense which the world entertained of him, as a prodigy unfit to be received among them on the usual terms of society, and as vindicating the wisdom of his purpose in withdrawing himself from among them. On the faith and sincerity of two persons alone, he seemed to rely implicitly--on that of his betrothed bride, and of a friend eminently gifted in personal accomplishments, who seemed, and indeed probably was, sincerely attached to him. He ought to have been so at least, for he was literally loaded with benefits by him whom you are now about to see. The parents of the subject of my story died within a short space of each other. Their death postponed the marriage, for which the day had been fixed. The lady did not seem greatly to mourn this delay,-- perhaps that was not to have been expected; but she intimated no change of intention, when, after a decent interval, a second day was named for their union. The friend of whom I spoke was then a constant resident at the Hall. In an evil hour, at the earnest request and entreaty of this friend, they joined a general party, where men of different political opinions were mingled, and where they drank deep. A quarrel ensued; the friend of the Recluse drew his sword with others, and was thrown down and disarmed by a more powerful antagonist. They fell in the struggle at the feet of the Recluse, who, maimed and truncated as his form appears, possesses, nevertheless, great strength, as well as violent passions. He caught up a sword, pierced the heart of his friend's antagonist, was tried, and his life, with difficulty, redeemed from justice at the expense of a year's close imprisonment, the punishment of manslaughter. The incident affected him most deeply, the more that the deceased was a man of excellent character, and had sustained gross insult and injury ere he drew his sword. I think, from that moment, I observed--I beg pardon--The fits of morbid sensibility which had tormented this unfortunate gentleman, were rendered henceforth more acute by remorse, which he, of all men, was least capable of having incurred, or of sustaining when it became his unhappy lot. His paroxysms of agony could not be concealed from the lady to whom he was betrothed; and it must be confessed they were of an alarming and fearful nature. He comforted himself, that, at the expiry of his imprisonment, he could form with his wife and friend a society, encircled by which he might dispense with more extensive communication with the world. He was deceived; before that term elapsed, his friend and his betrothed bride were man and wife. The effects of a shock so dreadful on an ardent temperament, a disposition already soured by bitter remorse, and loosened by the indulgence of a gloomy imagination from the rest of mankind, I cannot describe to you; it was as if the last cable at which the vessel rode had suddenly parted, and left her abandoned to all the wild fury of the tempest. He was placed under medical restraint. As a temporary measure this might have been justifiable; but his hard-hearted friend, who, in consequence of his marriage, was now his nearest ally, prolonged his confinement, in order to enjoy the management of his immense estates. There was one who owed his all to the sufferer, an humble friend, but grateful and faithful. By unceasing exertion, and repeated invocation of justice, he at length succeeded in obtaining his patron's freedom, and reinstatement in the management of his own property, to which was soon added that of his intended bride, who having died without male issue, her estates reverted to him, as heir of entail. But freedom and wealth were unable to restore the equipoise of his mind; to the former his grief made him indifferent--the latter only served him as far as it afforded him the means of indulging his strange and wayward fancy. He had renounced the Catholic religion, but perhaps some of its doctrines continued to influence a mind, over which remorse and misanthropy now assumed, in appearance, an unbounded authority. His life has since been that alternately of a pilgrim and a hermit, suffering the most severe privations, not indeed in ascetic devotion, but in abhorrence of mankind. Yet no man's words and actions have been at such a wide difference, nor has any hypocritical wretch ever been more ingenious in assigning good motives for his vile actions, than this unfortunate in reconciling to his abstract principles of misanthropy, a conduct which flows from his natural generosity and kindness of feeling."

"Still, Mr. Ratcliffe--still you describe the inconsistencies of a madman."

"By no means," replied Ratcliffe. "That the imagination of this gentleman is disordered, I will not pretend to dispute; I have already told you that it has sometimes broken out into paroxysms approaching to real mental alienation. But it is of his common state of mind that I speak; it is irregular, but not deranged; the shades are as gradual as those that divide the light of noonday from midnight. The courtier who ruins his fortune for the attainment of a title which can do him no good, or power of which he can make no suitable or creditable use, the miser who hoards his useless wealth, and the prodigal who squanders it, are all marked with a certain shade of insanity. To criminals who are guilty of enormities, when the temptation, to a sober mind, bears no proportion to the horror of the act, or the probability of detection and punishment, the same observation applies; and every violent passion, as well as anger, may be termed a short madness."

"This may be all good philosophy, Mr. Ratcliffe," answered Miss Vere; "but, excuse me, it by no means emboldens me to visit, at this late hour, a person whose extravagance of imagination you yourself can only palliate."

"Rather, then," said Ratcliffe, "receive my solemn assurances, that you do not incur the slightest danger. But what I have been hitherto afraid to mention for fear of alarming you is, that now when we are within sight of his retreat, for I can discover it through the twilight, I must go no farther with you; you must proceed alone."

"Alone?--I dare not."

"You must," continued Ratcliffe; "I will remain here and wait for you."

"You will not, then, stir from this place," said Miss Vere "yet the distance is so great, you could not hear me were I to cry for assistance."

"Fear nothing," said her guide; "or observe, at least, the utmost caution in stifling every expression of timidity. Remember that his predominant and most harassing apprehension arises from a consciousness of the hideousness of his appearance. Your path lies straight beside yon half-fallen willow; keep the left side of it; the marsh lies on the right. Farewell for a time. Remember the evil you are threatened with, and let it overcome at once your fears and scruples."

"Mr. Ratcliffe," said Isabella, "farewell; if you have deceived one so unfortunate as myself, you have for ever forfeited the fair character for probity and honour to which I have trusted."

"On my life--on my soul," continued Ratcliffe, raising his voice as the distance between them increased, "you are safe--perfectly safe."

CHAPTER XVI.

--'Twas time and griefs That framed him thus: Time, with his fairer hand, Offering the fortunes of his former days, The former man may make him.--Bring us to him, And chance it as it may. OLD PLAY.

The sounds of Ratcliffe's voice had died on Isabella's ear; but as she frequently looked back, it was some encouragement to her to discern his form now darkening in the gloom. Ere, however, she went much farther, she lost the object in the increasing shade. The last glimmer of the twilight placed her before the hut of the Solitary. She twice extended her hand to the door, and twice she withdrew it; and when she did at length make the effort, the knock did not equal in violence the throb of her own bosom. Her next effort was louder; her third was reiterated, for the fear of not obtaining the protection from which Ratcliffe promised so much, began to overpower the terrors of his presence from whom she was to request it. At length, as she still received no answer, she repeatedly called upon the Dwarf by his assumed name, and requested him to answer and open to her.

"What miserable being is reduced," said the appalling voice of the Solitary, "to seek refuge here? Go hence; when the heath- fowl need shelter, they seek it not in the nest of the night- raven."

"I come to you, father," said Isabella, "in my hour of adversity, even as you yourself commanded, when you promised your heart and your door should be open to my distress; but I fear--"

"Ha!" said the Solitary, "then thou art Isabella Vere? Give me a token that thou art she."

"I have brought you back the rose which you gave me; it has not had time to fade ere the hard fate you foretold has come upon me!"

"And if thou hast thus redeemed thy pledge," said the Dwarf, "I will not forfeit mine. The heart and the door that are shut against every other earthly being, shall be open to thee and to thy sorrows."

She heard him move in his hut, and presently afterwards strike a light. One by one, bolt and bar were then withdrawn, the heart of Isabella throbbing higher as these obstacles to their meeting were successively removed. The door opened, and the Solitary stood before her, his uncouth form and features illuminated by the iron lamp which he held in his hand.

"Enter, daughter of affliction," he said,--"enter the house of misery."

She entered, and observed, with a precaution which increased her trepidation, that the Recluse's first act, after setting the lamp upon the table, was to replace the numerous bolts which secured the door of his hut. She shrunk as she heard the noise which accompanied this ominous operation, yet remembered Ratcliffe's caution, and endeavoured to suppress all appearance of apprehension. The light of the lamp was weak and uncertain; but the Solitary, without taking immediate notice of Isabella, otherwise than by motioning her to sit down on a small settle beside the fireplace, made haste to kindle some dry furze, which presently cast a blaze through the cottage. Wooden shelves, which bore a few books, some bundles of dried herbs, and one or two wooden cups and platters, were on one side of the fire; on the other were placed some ordinary tools of field-labour, mingled with those used by mechanics. Where the bed should have been, there was a wooden frame, strewed with withered moss and rushes, the couch of the ascetic. The whole space of the cottage did not exceed ten feet by six within the walls; and its only furniture, besides what we have mentioned, was a table and two stools formed of rough deals.

Within these narrow precincts Isabella now found herself enclosed with a being, whose history had nothing to reassure her, and the fearful conformation of whose hideous countenance inspired an almost superstitious terror. He occupied the seat opposite to her, and dropping his huge and shaggy eyebrows over his piercing black eyes, gazed at her in silence, as if agitated by a variety of contending feelings. On the other side sate Isabella, pale as death, her long hair uncurled by the evening damps, and falling over her shoulders and breast, as the wet streamers droop from the mast when the storm has passed away, and left the vessel stranded on the beach. The Dwarf first broke the silence with the sudden, abrupt, and alarming question,--"Woman, what evil fate has brought thee hither?"

"My father's danger, and your own command," she replied faintly, but firmly.

"And you hope for aid from me?"

"If you can bestow it," she replied, still in the same tone of mild submission.

"And how should I possess that power?" continued the Dwarf, with a bitter sneer; "Is mine the form of a redresser of wrongs? Is this the castle in which one powerful enough to be sued to by a fair suppliant is likely to hold his residence? I but mocked thee, girl, when I said I would relieve thee."

"Then must I depart, and face my fate as I best may!"

"No!" said the Dwarf, rising and interposing between her and the door, and motioning to her sternly to resume her seat--"No! you leave me not in this way; we must have farther conference. Why should one being desire aid of another? Why should not each be sufficient to itself? Look round you--I, the most despised and most decrepit on Nature's common, have required sympathy and help from no one. These stones are of my own piling; these utensils I framed with my own hands; and with this"--and he laid his hand with a fierce smile on the long dagger which he always wore beneath his garment, and unsheathed it so far that the blade glimmered clear in the fire-light--"with this," he pursued, as he thrust the weapon back into the scabbard, "I can, if necessary, defend the vital spark enclosed in this poor trunk, against the fairest and strongest that shall threaten me with injury."

It was with difficulty Isabella refrained from screaming out aloud; but she DID refrain.

"This," continued the Recluse, "is the life of nature, solitary, self-sufficing, and independent. The wolf calls not the wolf to aid him in forming his den; and the vulture invites not another to assist her in striking down her prey."

"And when they are unable to procure themselves support," said Isabella, judiciously thinking that he would be most accessible to argument couched in his own metaphorical style, "what then is to befall them?"

"Let them starve, die, and be forgotten; it is the common lot of humanity."

"It is the lot of the wild tribes of nature," said Isabella, "but chiefly of those who are destined to support themselves by rapine, which brooks no partner; but it is not the law of nature in general; even the lower orders have confederacies for mutual defence. But mankind-- the race would perish did they cease to aid each other.--From the time that the mother binds the child's head, till the moment that some kind assistant wipes the death- damp from the brow of the dying, we cannot exist without mutual help. All, therefore, that need aid, have right to ask it of their fellow-mortals; no one who has the power of granting can refuse it without guilt."

"And in this simple hope, poor maiden," said the Solitary, "thou hast come into the desert, to seek one whose wish it were that the league thou hast spoken of were broken for ever, and that, in very truth, the whole race should perish? Wert thou not frightened?"

"Misery," said Isabella, firmly, "is superior to fear."

"Hast thou not heard it said in thy mortal world, that I have leagued myself with other powers, deformed to the eye and malevolent to the human race as myself? Hast thou not heard this--And dost thou seek my cell at midnight?"

"The Being I worship supports me against such idle fears," said Isabella; but the increasing agitation of her bosom belied the affected courage which her words expressed.

"Ho! ho!" said the Dwarf, "thou vauntest thyself a philosopher? Yet, shouldst thou not have thought of the danger of intrusting thyself, young and beautiful, in the power of one so spited against humanity, as to place his chief pleasure in defacing, destroying, and degrading her fairest works?"

Isabella, much alarmed, continued to answer with firmness, "Whatever injuries you may have sustained in the world, you are incapable of revenging them on one who never wronged you, nor, wilfully, any other."

"Ay, but, maiden," he continued, his dark eyes flashing with an expression of malignity which communicated itself to his wild and distorted features, "revenge is the hungry wolf, which asks only to tear flesh and lap blood. Think you the lamb's plea of innocence would be listened to by him?"

"Man!" said Isabella, rising, and expressing herself with much dignity, "I fear not the horrible ideas with which you would impress me. I cast them from me with disdain. Be you mortal or fiend, you would not offer injury to one who sought you as a suppliant in her utmost need. You would not--you durst not."

"Thou say'st truly, maiden," rejoined the Solitary; "I dare not --I would not. Begone to thy dwelling. Fear nothing with which they threaten thee. Thou hast asked my protection--thou shalt find it effectual."

"But, father, this very night I have consented to wed the man that I abhor, or I must put the seal to my father's ruin."

"This night?--at what hour?"

"Ere midnight."

"And twilight," said the Dwarf, "has already passed away. But fear nothing, there is ample time to protect thee."

"And my father?" continued Isabella, in a suppliant tone.

"Thy father," replied the Dwarf, "has been, and is, my most bitter enemy. But fear not; thy virtue shall save him. And now, begone; were I to keep thee longer by me, I might again fall into the stupid dreams concerning human worth from which I have been so fearfully awakened. But fear nothing--at the very foot of the altar I will redeem thee. Adieu, time presses, and I must act!"

He led her to the door of the hut, which he opened for her departure. She remounted her horse, which had been feeding in the outer enclosure, and pressed him forward by the light of the moon, which was now rising, to the spot where she had left Ratcliffe.

"Have you succeeded?" was his first eager question.

"I have obtained promises from him to whom you sent me; but how can he possibly accomplish them?"

"Thank God!" said Ratcliffe; "doubt not his power to fulfil his promise."

At this moment a shrill whistle was heard to resound along the heath.

"Hark!" said Ratcliffe, "he calls me--Miss Vere, return home, and leave unbolted the postern-door of the garden; to that which opens on the back-stairs I have a private key."

A second whistle was heard, yet more shrill and prolonged than the first.

"I come, I come," said Ratcliffe; and setting spurs to his horse, rode over the heath in the direction of the Recluse's hut. Miss Vere returned to the castle, the mettle of the animal on which she rode, and her own anxiety of mind, combining to accelerate her journey.

She obeyed Ratcliffe's directions, though without well apprehending their purpose, and leaving her horse at large in a paddock near the garden, hurried to her own apartment, which she reached without observation. She now unbolted her door, and rang her bell for lights. Her father appeared along with the servant who answered her summons.

"He had been twice," he said, "listening at her door during the two hours that had elapsed since he left her, and, not hearing her speak, had become apprehensive that she was taken ill."

"And now, my dear father," she said, "permit me to claim the promise you so kindly gave; let the last moments of freedom which I am to enjoy be mine without interruption; and protract to the last moment the respite which is allowed me."

"I will," said her father; "nor shall you be again interrupted. But this disordered dress--this dishevelled hair--do not let me find you thus when I call on you again; the sacrifice, to be beneficial, must be voluntary."

"Must it be so?" she replied; "then fear not, my father! the victim shall be adorned."

CHAPTER XVII.

This looks not like a nuptial. MUCH ADO ABOUT NOTHING.

The chapel in the castle of Ellieslaw, destined to be the scene of this ill-omened union, was a building of much older date than the castle itself, though that claimed considerable antiquity. Before the wars between England and Scotland had become so common and of such long duration, that the buildings along both sides of the Border were chiefly dedicated to warlike purposes, there had been a small settlement of monks at Ellieslaw, a dependency, it is believed by antiquaries, on the rich Abbey of Jedburgh. Their possessions had long passed away under the changes introduced by war and mutual ravage. A feudal castle had arisen on the ruin of their cells, and their chapel was included in its precincts.

The edifice, in its round arches and massive pillars, the simplicity of which referred their date to what has been called the Saxon architecture, presented at all times a dark and sombre appearance, and had been frequently used as the cemetery of the family of the feudal lords, as well as formerly of the monastic brethren. But it looked doubly gloomy by the effect of the few and smoky torches which were used to enlighten it on the present occasion, and which, spreading a glare of yellow light in their immediate vicinity, were surrounded beyond by a red and purple halo reflected from their own smoke, and beyond that again by a zone of darkness which magnified the extent of the chapel, while it rendered it impossible for the eye to ascertain its limits. Some injudicious ornaments, adopted in haste for the occasion, rather added to the dreariness of the scene. Old fragments of tapestry, torn from the walls of other apartments, had been hastily and partially disposed around those of the chapel, and mingled inconsistently with scutcheons and funeral emblems of the dead, which they elsewhere exhibited. On each side of the stone altar was a monument, the appearance of which formed an equally strange contrast. On the one was the figure, in stone, of some grim hermit, or monk, who had died in the odour of sanctity; he was represented as recumbent, in his cowl and scapulaire, with his face turned upward as in the act of devotion, and his hands folded, from which his string of beads was dependent. On the other side was a tomb, in the Italian taste, composed of the most beautiful statuary marble, and accounted a model of modern art. It was erected to the memory of Isabella's mother, the late Mrs. Vere of Ellieslaw, who was represented as in a dying posture, while a weeping cherub, with eyes averted, seemed in the act of extinguishing a dying lamp as emblematic of her speedy dissolution. It was, indeed, a masterpiece of art, but misplaced in the rude vault to which it had been consigned. Many were surprised, and even scandalized, that Ellieslaw, not remarkable for attention to his lady while alive, should erect after her death such a costly mausoleum in affected sorrow; others cleared him from the imputation of hypocrisy, and averred that the monument had been constructed under the direction and at the sole expense of Mr. Ratcliffe.

Before these monuments the wedding guests were assembled. They were few in number; for many had left the castle to prepare for the ensuing political explosion, and Ellieslaw was, in the circumstances of the case, far from being desirous to extend invitations farther than to those near relations whose presence the custom of the country rendered indispensable. Next to the altar stood Sir Frederick Langley, dark, moody, and thoughtful, even beyond his wont, and near him, Mareschal, who was to play the part of bridesman, as it was called. The thoughtless humour of this young gentleman, on which he never deigned to place the least restraint, added to the cloud which overhung the brow of the bridegroom

"The bride is not yet come out of her chamber," he whispered to Sir Frederick; "I trust that we must not have recourse to the violent expedients of the Romans which I read of at College. It would be hard upon my pretty cousin to be run away with twice in two days, though I know none better worth such a violent compliment."

Sir Frederick attempted to turn a deaf ear to this discourse, humming a tune, and looking another may, but Mareschal proceeded in the same wild manner.

"This delay is hard upon Dr. Hobbler, who was disturbed to accelerate preparations for this joyful event when he had successfully extracted the cork of his third bottle. I hope you will keep him free of the censure of his superiors, for I take it this is beyond canonical hours.--But here come Ellieslaw and my pretty cousin--prettier than ever, I think, were it not she seems so faint and so deadly pale--Hark ye, Sir Knight, if she says not YES with right good-will, it shall be no wedding, for all that has come and gone yet."

"No wedding, sir?" returned Sir Frederick, in a loud whisper, the tone of which indicated that his angry feelings were suppressed with difficulty.

"No--no marriage," replied Mareschal, "there's my hand and glove on't."

Sir Frederick Langley took his hand, and as he wrung it hard, said in a lower whisper, "Mareschal, you shall answer this," and then flung his hand from him.

"That I will readily do," said Mareschal, "for never word escaped my lips that my hand was not ready to guarantee.- So, speak up, my pretty cousin, and tell me if it be your free will and unbiassed resolution to accept of this gallant knight for your lord and husband; for if you have the tenth part of a scruple upon the subject, fall back, fall edge, he shall not have you."

"Are you mad, Mr. Mareschal?" said Ellieslaw, who, having been this young man's guardian during his minority, often employed a tone of authority to him. "Do you suppose I would drag my daughter to the foot of the altar, were it not her own choice?"

"Tut, Ellieslaw," retorted the young gentleman, "never tell me of the contrary; her eyes are full of tears, and her cheeks are whiter than her white dress. I must insist, in the name of common humanity, that the ceremony be adjourned till to-morrow."

"She shall tell you herself, thou incorrigible intermeddler in what concerns thee not, that it is her wish the ceremony should go on--Is it not, Isabella, my dear?"

"It is," said Isabella, half fainting--"since there is no help, either in God or man."

The first word alone was distinctly audible. Mareschal shrugged up his shoulders and stepped back. Ellieslaw led, or rather supported, his daughter to the altar. Sir Frederick moved forward and placed himself by her side. The clergyman opened his prayer-book, and looked to Mr. Vere for the signal to commence the service.

"Proceed," said the latter.

But a voice, as if issuing from the tomb of his deceased wife, called, in such loud and harsh accents as awakened every echo in the vaulted chapel, "Forbear!"

All were mute and motionless, till a distant rustle, and the clash of swords, or something resembling it, was heard from the remote apartments. It ceased almost instantly.

"What new device is this?" said Sir Frederick, fiercely, eyeing Ellieslaw and Mareschal with a glance of malignant suspicion.

"It can be but the frolic of some intemperate guest," said Ellieslaw, though greatly confounded; "we must make large allowances for the excess of this evening's festivity. Proceed with the service."

Before the clergyman could obey, the same prohibition which they had before heard, was repeated from the same spot. The female attendants screamed, and fled from the chapel; the gentlemen laid their hands on their swords. Ere the first moment of surprise had passed by, the Dwarf stepped from behind the monument, and placed himself full in front of Mr. Vere. The effect of so strange and hideous an apparition in such a place and in such circumstances, appalled all present, but seemed to annihilate the Laird of Ellieslaw, who, dropping his daughter's arm, staggered against the nearest pillar, and, clasping it with his hands as if for support, laid his brow against the column.

"Who is this fellow?" said Sir Frederick; "and what does he mean by this intrusion?"

"It is one who comes to tell you," said the Dwarf, with the peculiar acrimony which usually marked his manner, "that, in marrying that young lady, you wed neither the heiress of Ellieslaw, nor of Mauley Hall, nor of Polverton, nor of one furrow of land, unless she marries with MY consent; and to thee that consent shall never be given. Down--down on thy knees, and thank Heaven that thou art prevented from wedding qualities with which thou hast no concern--portionless truth, virtue, and innocence--thou, base ingrate," he continued, addressing himself to Ellieslaw, "what is thy wretched subterfuge now? Thou, who wouldst sell thy daughter to relieve thee from danger, as in famine thou wouldst have slain and devoured her to preserve thy own vile life!--Ay, hide thy face with thy hands; well mayst thou blush to look on him whose body thou didst consign to chains, his hand to guilt, and his soul to misery. Saved once more by the virtue of her who calls thee father, go hence, and may the pardon and benefits I confer on thee prove literal coals of fire, till thy brain is seared and scorched like mine!"

Ellieslaw left the chapel with a gesture of mute despair.

"Follow him, Hubert Ratcliffe," said the Dwarf, "and inform him of his destiny. He will rejoice--for to breathe air and to handle gold is to him happiness,"

"I understand nothing of all this," said Sir Frederick Langley; "but we are here a body of gentlemen in arms and authority for King James; and whether you really, sir, be that Sir Edward Mauley, who has been so long supposed dead in confinement, or whether you be an impostor assuming his name and title, we will use the freedom of detaining you, till your appearance here, at this moment, is better accounted for; we will have no spies among us--Seize on him, my friends."

But the domestics shrunk back in doubt and alarm. Sir Frederick himself stepped forward towards the Recluse, as if to lay hands on his person, when his progress was suddenly stopped by the glittering point of a partisan, which the sturdy hand of Hobbie Elliot presented against his bosom.

"I'll gar daylight shine through ye, if ye offer to steer him!" said the stout Borderer; "stand back, or I'll strike ye through! Naebody shall lay a finger on Elshie; he's a canny neighbourly man, aye ready to make a friend help; and, though ye may think him a lamiter, yet, grippie for grippie, friend, I'll wad a wether he'll make the bluid spin frae under your nails. He's a teugh carle Elshie! he grips like a smith's vice."

"What has brought you here, Elliot?" said Mareschal; "who called on you for interference?"

"Troth, Mareschal-Wells," answered Hobbie, "I am just come here, wi' twenty or thretty mair o' us, in my ain name and the King's --or Queen's, ca' they her? and Canny Elshie's into the bargain, to keep the peace, and pay back some ill usage Ellieslaw has gien me. A bonny breakfast the loons gae me the ither morning, and him at the bottom on't; and trow ye I wasna ready to supper him up?--Ye needna lay your hands on your swords, gentlemen, the house is ours wi' little din; for the doors were open, and there had been ower muckle punch amang your folk; we took their swords and pistols as easily as ye wad shiel pea-cods."

Mareschal rushed out, and immediately re-entered the chapel.

"By Heaven! it is true, Sir Frederick; the house is filled with armed men, and our drunken beasts are all disarmed. Draw, and let us fight our way."

"Binna rash--binna rash," exclaimed Hobbie; "hear me a bit, hear me a bit. We mean ye nae harm; but, as ye are in arms for King James, as ye ca' him, and the prelates, we thought it right to keep up the auld neighbour war, and stand up for the t'other ane and the Kirk; but we'll no hurt a hair o' your heads, if ye like to gang hame quietly. And it will be your best way, for there's sure news come frae Loudoun, that him they ca' Bang, or Byng, or what is't, has bang'd the French ships and the new king aff the coast however; sae ye had best bide content wi' auld Nanse for want of a better Queen."

Ratcliffe, who at this moment entered, confirmed these accounts so unfavourable to the Jacobite interest. Sir Frederick, almost instantly, and without taking leave of any one, left the castle, with such of his attendants as were able to follow him.

"And what will you do, Mr. Mareschal?" said Ratcliffe.

"Why, faith," answered he, smiling, "I hardly know; my spirit is too great, and my fortune too small, for me to follow the example of the doughty bridegroom. It is not in my nature, and it is hardly worth my while."

"Well, then, disperse your men, and remain quiet, and this will be overlooked, as there has been no overt act."

"Hout, ay," said Elliot, "just let byganes be byganes, and a' friends again; deil ane I bear malice at but Westburnflat, and I hae gien him baith a het skin and a cauld ane. I hadna changed three blows of the broadsword wi' him before he lap the window into the castle-moat, and swattered through it like a wild-duck. He's a clever fallow, indeed! maun kilt awa wi' ae bonny lass in the morning, and another at night, less wadna serve him! but if he disna kilt himsell out o' the country, I'se kilt him wi' a tow, for the Castleton meeting's clean blawn ower; his friends will no countenance him."

During the general confusion, Isabella had thrown herself at the feet of her kinsman, Sir Edward Mauley, for so we must now call the Solitary, to express at once her gratitude, and to beseech forgiveness for her father. The eyes of all began to be fixed on them, as soon as their own agitation and the bustle of the attendants had somewhat abated. Miss Vere kneeled beside the tomb of her mother, to whose statue her features exhibited a marked resemblance. She held the hand of the Dwarf, which she kissed repeatedly and bathed with tears. He stood fixed and motionless, excepting that his eyes glanced alternately on the marble figure and the living suppliant. At length, the large drops which gathered on his eye-lashes compelled him to draw his hand across them.

"I thought," he said, "that tears and I had done; but we shed them at our birth, and their spring dries not until we are in our graves. But no melting of the heart shall dissolve my resolution. I part here, at once, and for ever, with all of which the memory" (looking to the tomb), "or the presence" (he pressed Isabella's hand), "is dear to me.--Speak not to me! attempt not to thwart my determination! it will avail nothing; you will hear of and see this lump of deformity no more. To you I shall be dead ere I am actually in my grave, and you will think of me as of a friend disencumbered from the toils and crimes of existence."

He kissed Isabella on the forehead, impressed another kiss on the brow of the statue by which she knelt, and left the chapel followed by Ratcliffe. Isabella, almost exhausted by the emotions of the day, was carried to her apartment by her women. Most of the other guests dispersed, after having separately endeavoured to impress on all who would listen to them their disapprobation of the plots formed against the government, or their regret for having engaged in them. Hobbie Elliot assumed the command of the castle for the night, and mounted a regular guard. He boasted not a little of the alacrity with which his friends and he had obeyed a hasty summons received from Elshie through the faithful Ratcliffe. And it was a lucky chance, he said, that on that very day they had got notice that Westburnflat did not intend to keep his tryste at Castleton, but to hold them at defiance; so that a considerable party had assembled at the Heughfoot, with the intention of paying a visit to the robber's tower on the ensuing morning, and their course was easily directed to Ellieslaw Castle.

CHAPTER XVIII.

--Last scene of all, To close this strange eventful history. AS YOU LIKE IT.

On the next morning, Mr. Ratcliffe presented Miss Vere with a letter from her father, of which the following is the tenor:--

"MY DEAREST CHILD, The malice of a persecuting government will compel me, for my own safety, to retreat abroad, and to remain for some time in foreign parts. I do not ask you to accompany, or follow me; you will attend to my interest and your own more effectually by remaining where you are. It is unnecessary to enter into a minute detail concerning the causes of the strange events which yesterday took place. I think I have reason to complain of the usage I have received from Sir Edward Mauley, who is your nearest kinsman by the mother's side; but as he has declared you his heir, and is to put you in immediate possession of a large part of his fortune, I account it a full atonement. I am aware he has never forgiven the preference which your mother gave to my addresses, instead of complying with the terms of a sort of family compact, which absurdly and tyrannically destined her to wed her deformed relative. The shock was even sufficient to unsettle his wits (which, indeed, were never over-well arranged), and I had, as the husband of his nearest kinswoman and heir, the delicate task of taking care of his person and property, until he was reinstated in the management of the latter by those who, no doubt, thought they were doing him justice; although, if some parts of his subsequent conduct be examined, it will appear that he ought, for his own sake, to have been left under the influence of a mild and salutary restraint.

"In one particular, however, he showed a sense of the ties of blood, as well as of his own frailty; for while he sequestered himself closely from the world, under various names and disguises, and insisted on spreading a report of his own death (in which to gratify him I willingly acquiesced), he left at my disposal the rents of a great proportion of his estates, and especially all those, which, having belonged to your mother, reverted to him as a male fief. In this he may have thought that he was acting with extreme generosity, while, in the opinion of all impartial men, he will only be considered as having fulfilled a natural obligation, seeing that, in justice, if not in strict law, you must be considered as the heir of your mother, and I as your legal administrator. Instead, therefore, of considering myself as loaded with obligations to Sir Edward on this account, I think I had reason to complain that these remittances were only doled out to me at the pleasure of Mr. Ratcliffe, who, moreover, exacted from me mortgages over my paternal estate of Ellieslaw for any sums which I required as an extra advance; and thus may be said to have insinuated himself into the absolute management and control of my property. Or, if all this seeming friendship was employed by Sir Edward for the purpose of obtaining a complete command of my affairs, and acquiring the power of ruining me at his pleasure, I feel myself, I must repeat, still less bound by the alleged obligation.

"About the autumn of last year, as I understand, either his own crazed imagination, or the accomplishment of some such scheme as I have hinted, brought him down to this country. His alleged motive, it seems, was a desire of seeing a monument which he had directed to be raised in the chapel over the tomb of your mother. Mr. Ratcliffe, who at this time had done me the honour to make my house his own, had the complaisance to introduce him secretly into the chapel. The consequence, as he informs me, was a frenzy of several hours, during which he fled into the neighbouring moors, in one of the wildest spots of which he chose, when he was somewhat recovered, to fix his mansion, and set up for a sort of country empiric, a character which, even in his best days, he was fond of assuming. It is remarkable, that, instead of informing me of these circumstances, that I might have had the relative of my late wife taken such care of as his calamitous condition required, Mr. Ratcliffe seems to have had such culpable indulgence for his irregular plans as to promise and even swear secrecy concerning them. He visited Sir Edward often, and assisted in the fantastic task he had taken upon him of constructing a hermitage. Nothing they appear to have dreaded more than a discovery of their intercourse.

"The ground was open in every direction around, and a small subterranean cave, probably sepulchral, which their researches had detected near the great granite pillar, served to conceal Ratcliffe, when any one approached his master. I think you will be of opinion, my love, that this secrecy must have had some strong motive. It is also remarkable, that while I thought my unhappy friend was residing among the Monks of La Trappe, he should have been actually living, for many months, in this bizarre disguise, within five miles of my house, and obtaining regular information of my most private movements, either by Ratcliffe, or through Westburnflat or others, whom he had the means to bribe to any extent. He makes it a crime against me that I endeavoured to establish your marriage with Sir Frederick. I acted for the best; but if Sir Edward Mauley thought otherwise, why did he not step manfully forward, express his own purpose of becoming a party to the settlements, and take that interest which he is entitled to claim in you as heir to his great property?

"Even now, though your rash and eccentric relation is somewhat tardy in announcing his purpose, I am far from opposing my authority against his wishes, although the person he desires you to regard as your future husband be young Earnscliff; the very last whom I should have thought likely to be acceptable to him, considering a certain fatal event. But I give my free and hearty consent, providing the settlements are drawn in such an irrevocable form as may secure my child from suffering by that state of dependence, and that sudden and causeless revocation of allowances, of which I have so much reason to complain. Of Sir Frederick Langley, I augur, you will hear no more. He is not likely to claim the hand of a dowerless maiden. I therefore commit you, my dear Isabella, to the wisdom of Providence and to your own prudence, begging you to lose no time in securing those advantages, which the fickleness of your kinsman has withdrawn from me to shower upon you.

"Mr. Ratcliffe mentioned Sir Edward's intention to settle a considerable sum upon me yearly, for my maintenance in foreign parts; but this my heart is too proud to accept from him. I told him I had a dear child, who, while in affluence herself, would never suffer me to be in poverty. I thought it right to intimate this to him pretty roundly, that whatever increase be settled upon you, it may be calculated so as to cover this necessary and natural encumbrance. I shall willingly settle upon you the castle and manor of Ellieslaw, to show my parental affection and disinterested zeal for promoting your settlement in life. The annual interest of debts charged on the estate somewhat exceeds the income, even after a reasonable rent has been put upon the mansion and mains. But as all the debts are in the person of Mr. Ratcliffe, as your kinsman's trustee, he will not be a troublesome creditor. And here I must make you aware, that though I have to complain of Mr. Ratcliffe's conduct to me personally, I, nevertheless, believe him a just and upright man, with whom you may safely consult on your affairs, not to mention that to cherish his good opinion will be the best way to retain that of your kinsman. Remember me to Marchie--I hope he will not be troubled on account of late matters. I will write more fully from the Continent. Meanwhile, I rest your loving father, RICHARD VERE."

The above letter throws the only additional light which we have been able to procure upon the earlier part of our story. It was Hobbie's opinion, and may be that of most of our readers,that the Recluse of Mucklestane-Moor had but a kind of a gleaming, or twilight understanding; and that he had neither very clear views as to what he himself wanted, nor was apt to pursue his ends by the clearest and most direct means; so that to seek the clew of his conduct, was likened, by Hobbie, to looking for a straight path through a common, over which are a hundred devious tracks, but not one distinct line of road.

When Isabella had perused the letter, her first enquiry was after her father. He had left the castle, she was informed, early in the morning, after a long interview with Mr. Ratcliffe, and was already far on his way to the next port, where he might expect to find shipping for the Continent.

"Where was Sir Edward Mauley?"

No one had seen the Dwarf since the eventful scene of the preceding evening.

"Odd, if onything has befa'en puir Elshie," said Hobbie Elliot, "I wad rather I were harried ower again."

He immediately rode to his dwelling, and the remaining she-goat came bleating to meet him, for her milking time was long past. The Solitary was nowhere to be seen; his door, contrary to wont, was open, his fire extinguished, and the whole hut was left in the state which it exhibited on Isabella's visit to him. It was pretty clear that the means of conveyance which had brought the Dwarf to Ellieslaw on the preceding evening, had removed him from it to some other place of abode. Hobbie returned disconsolate to the castle.

"I am doubting we hae lost Canny Elshie for gude an' a'."

"You have indeed," said Ratcliffe, producing a paper, which he put into Hobbie's hands; "but read that, and you will perceive you have been no loser by having known him."

It was a short deed of gift, by which "Sir Edward Mauley, otherwise called Elshender the Recluse, endowed Halbert or Hobbie Elliot, and Grace Armstrong, in full property, with a considerable sum borrowed by Elliot from him."

Hobbie's joy was mingled with feelings which brought tears down his rough cheeks.

"It's a queer thing," he said; "but I canna joy in the gear, unless I kend the puir body was happy that gave it me."

"Next to enjoying happiness ourselves," said Ratcliffe, "is the consciousness of having bestowed it on others. Had all my master's benefits been conferred like the present, what a different return would they have produced! But the indiscriminate profusion that would glut avarice, or supply prodigality, neither does good, nor is rewarded by gratitude. It is sowing the wind to reap the whirlwind."

"And that wad be a light har'st," said Hobbie; "but, wi' my young leddie's leave, I wad fain take down Eishie's skeps o' bees, and set them in Grace's bit flower yard at the Heugh-foot--they shall ne'er be smeekit by ony o' huz. And the puir goat, she would be negleckit about a great toun like this; and she could feed bonnily on our lily lea by the burn side, and the hounds wad ken her in a day's time, and never fash her, and Grace wad milk her ilka morning wi' her ain hand, for Elshie's sake; for though he was thrawn and cankered in his converse, he likeit dumb creatures weel."

Hobbie's requests were readily granted, not without some wonder at the natural delicacy of feeling which pointed out to him this mode of displaying his gratitude. He was delighted when Ratcliffe informed him that his benefactor should not remain ignorant of the care which he took of his favourite.

"And mind be sure and tell him that grannie and the titties, and, abune a', Grace and mysell, are weel and thriving, and that it's a' his doing--that canna but please him, ane wad think."

And Elliot and the family at Heugh-foot were, and continued to be, as fortunate and happy as his undaunted honesty, tenderness, and gallantry so well merited.

All bar between the marriage of Earnscliff and Isabella was now removed, and the settlements which Ratcliffe produced on the part of Sir Edward Mauley, might have satisfied the cupidity of Ellieslaw himself. But Miss Vere and Ratcliffe thought it unnecessary to mention to Earnscliff that one great motive of Sir Edward, in thus loading the young pair with benefits, was to expiate his having, many years before, shed the blood of his father in a hasty brawl. If it be true, as Ratcliffe asserted, that the Dwarf's extreme misanthropy seemed to relax somewhat, under the consciousness of having diffused happiness among so many, the recollection of this circumstance might probably be one of his chief motives for refusing obstinately ever to witness their state of contentment.

Mareschal hunted, shot, and drank claret--tired of the country, went abroad, served three campaigns, came home, and married Lucy Ilderton.

Years fled over the heads of Earnscliff and his wife, and found and left them contented and happy. The scheming ambition of Sir Frederick Langley engaged him in the unfortunate insurrection of 1715. He was made prisoner at Preston, in Lancashire, with the Earl of Derwentwater, and others. His defence, and the dying speech which he made at his execution, may be found in the State Trials. Mr. Vere, supplied by his daughter with an ample income, continued to reside abroad, engaged deeply in the affair of Law's bank during the regency of the Duke of Orleans, and was at one time supposed to be immensely rich. But, on the bursting of that famous bubble, he was so much chagrined at being again reduced to a moderate annuity (although he saw thousands of his companions in misfortune absolutely starving), that vexation of mind brought on a paralytic stroke, of which he died, after lingering under its effects a few weeks.

Willie of Westburnflat fled from the wrath of Hobbie Elliot, as his betters did from the pursuit of the law. His patriotism urged him to serve his country abroad, while his reluctance to leave his native soil pressed him rather to remain in the beloved island, and collect purses, watches, and rings on the highroads at home. Fortunately for him, the first impulse prevailed, and he joined the army under Marlborough; obtained a commission to which he was recommended by his services in collecting cattle for the commissariat; returned home after many years, with some money (how come by Heaven only knows),--demolished the peel-house at

Westburnflat, and built, in its stead, a high narrow ONSTEAD, of three stories, with a chimney at each end--drank brandy with the neighbours, whom, in his younger days, he had plundered--died in his bed, and is recorded upon his tombstone at Kirkwhistle (still extant), as having played all the parts of a brave soldier, a discreet neighbour, and a sincere Christian.

Mr. Ratcliffe resided usually with the family at Ellieslaw, but regularly every spring and autumn he absented himself for about a month. On the direction and purpose of his periodical journey he remained steadily silent; but it was well understood that he was then in attendance on his unfortunate patron. At length, on his return from one of these visits, his grave countenance, and deep mourning dress, announced to the Ellieslaw family that their benefactor was no more. Sir Edward's death made no addition to their fortune, for he had divested himself of his property during his lifetime, and chiefly in their favour. Ratcliffe, his sole confidant, died at a good old age, but without ever naming the place to which his master had finally retired, or the manner of his death, or the place of his burial. It was supposed that on all these particulars his patron had enjoined him strict secrecy.

The sudden disappearance of Elshie from his extraordinary hermitage corroborated the reports which the common people had spread concerning him. Many believed that, having ventured to enter a consecrated building, contrary to his paction with the Evil One, he had been bodily carried off while on his return to his cottage; but most are of opinion that he only disappeared for a season, and continues to be seen from time to time among the hills. And retaining, according to custom, a more vivid recollection of his wild and desperate language, than of the benevolent tendency of most of his actions, he is usually identified with the malignant demon called the Man of the Moors, whose feats were quoted by Mrs. Elliot to her grandsons; and, accordingly, is generally represented as bewitching the sheep, causing the ewes to KEB, that is, to cast their lambs, or seen loosening the impending wreath of snow to precipitate its weight on such as take shelter, during the storm, beneath the bank of a torrent, or under the shelter of a deep glen. In short, the evils most dreaded and deprecated by the inhabitants of that pastoral country, are ascribed to the agency of the BLACK DWARF.

Printed in the United Kingdom
by Lightning Source UK Ltd.
113756UKS00001B/172